WINTER'S BULLET

WINTER'S BULLET

WILLIAM OSBORNE

Chicken House

SCHOLASTIC INC. | NEW YORK

ISBN 978-1-338-03301-4

10 9 8 7 6 5 4 3 2 1   16 17 18 19 20

Printed in the U.S.A.   40
First printing 2016
Book design by Yaffa Jaskoll

To the Osborne family

"We have a bomb with a working that will astonish the whole world." —Adolf Hitler at a meeting with Mussolini, July 1944

"Save one life, save the world." —The Talmud

1

It was just before dawn when General Müller, head of the Gestapo, arrived at the Adlerhorst.

The Führer had based himself at this medieval German castle to direct his daring offensive against the Americans and British in the forests of the Ardennes. But news from the front was bleak: The German army had ground to a halt, and the enemy was counterattacking with overwhelming force.

After six years, the unthinkable was happening: The Third Reich was losing the war.

General Müller stared out at the darkness beyond the car window, his mind racing. At least they still had Operation Black Sun, he thought. It was both their last hope and the best hope of victory. And he was here to report on its progress to Hitler himself. Everything was ready, he told himself: the secret airbase near Amsterdam; the friends in South America; the sea trial; the weapon itself . . .

After a series of checkpoints, his Mercedes pulled to a halt in the castle's large courtyard. A series of blast-proof concrete bunkers had been built beyond it, cleverly disguised to look like small cottages. Müller climbed out and stretched.

A sense of defeat seemed to hang in the foggy air. There was a muted silence to the staff officers who passed him, saluting perfunctorily. The atmosphere wasn't helped by the still-smoldering remains of the village church and several cottages that had been hit by Allied bombs a few days earlier. The Führer had been assured it was coincidental—his whereabouts were a closely guarded secret since the assassination attempt last July—but nevertheless, it added to the sense of a tightening net.

Müller reached Haus 2. A uniformed valet opened the door and took his winter coat and hat, then escorted him to an ante-chamber outside Hitler's situation room. The place had been decorated to resemble an Alpine lodge; it was very cozy, Müller thought, *sehr gemütlich*.

Reichsleiter Bormann was standing in front of a fire warming his legs. He didn't move his squat, paunchy body to greet Müller, just fixed him with his black eyes.

"So, Müller, what is your report on Operation Black Sun?" he said. "The Führer is anxious to hear it."

"Everything is proceeding to plan and on schedule." Müller pulled off his gloves slowly, finger by finger.

"And the bomb?"

"It will be shipped to the Amsterdam airbase in time."

Bormann merely nodded.

The two men waited in silence for the Führer to conclude the morning briefing of the Ardennes offensive. When the last of the tense-faced generals had departed, Müller and Bormann stepped inside and the doors slammed shut behind them.

They snapped salutes to the Führer, who waved them away.

"I'd like some good news for a change, Müller," he said. "My generals continue to thwart all my best endeavors." Though he looked thin and his hair was lank, there was still, Müller thought, a sense of burning energy.

"Of course—" he began before Bormann the sycophant interrupted him.

"General Müller reports that all aspects of Operation Black Sun are in place."

Müller watched as Hitler nodded, mulling it over.

"This bomb . . ."

"Here, *mein Führer* . . ." Bormann quickly laid out a map in front of Hitler, who studied it carefully with a large magnifying glass.

"New York?"

"*Ja, mein Führer.* Observe . . ." Bormann jabbed his middle finger at a series of concentric rings. "Central Park. The first two rings spell total annihilation. Everything reduced to dust."

The Führer stared at the two rings, the second one extending well beyond the island of Manhattan. "So this atom-splitting weapon will work," he said eventually. "Incredible."

"Indeed, *mein Führer*," said Bormann. "With this weapon you can win the war in one stroke. The genius of German technology will be the Fatherland's salvation."

The Führer threw down the magnifying glass and stabbed an accusing finger at the two men. "Didn't I tell you," he said, "didn't I tell the German nation to keep the faith, that we would triumph over whatever the Americans and Bolsheviks threw at us?"

His voice grew louder and stronger as he spoke. Müller noticed a fleck of spit form in the corner of his mouth. There was silence for a moment. Hitler closed his eyes briefly, then opened them.

"If the sea trial of the weapon is successful then we move immediately—in three days. Müller, you will fetch my baggage."

Müller frowned, not understanding. "Your baggage, *mein Führer*?"

"Frau Braun, she is staying at the Berghof. Bring the sister too—she will want some company in Argentina, no doubt."

"*Ja, mein Führer.*"

"And my special gift that I promised our Argentinian friend? The stone?"

"The stone—" Bormann began, but this time Müller interrupted him.

"Everything will be in order by the time we leave, *mein Führer.*"

Hitler frowned. "See that it is. I gave my word to the señorita."

Müller saluted and the Führer planted his hands on his hips, his eyes bright.

"Take heart, gentlemen, the real war is just about to start! This weapon—this wonder weapon—will rain death on any city we choose: first New York, then Moscow, and finally Churchill's London. We will bomb them all back into the Stone Age!"

2

It was a little after seven in the morning, still dark with a bone-chilling wind blowing through the city of Amsterdam. It sent the snow that had settled on the frozen canals dancing back up into the sky. Through this blizzard a figure suddenly appeared, racing along the surface of the ice. His skates were singing, his torso bent forward against the wind.

Tygo Winter, fifteen years old last June, was this lone skater shooting past the canal boats and barges seized in the ice. He was bundled up against the elements, a ratty old woolen balaclava over his head with a felt hat on top for good measure, secured with twine. His brown eyes, so dark you could not distinguish the iris from the pupil, squinted ahead through the driving snow.

He had reached the end of the first canal and turned a sharp right into the next, larger this time but still frozen solid.

It was only the third time he had adopted this method of reaching his place of work, and he realized how weak and unfit he had become since the winter of hunger had begun in Amsterdam. His legs felt like jelly and his knees were on fire, but he pressed on as fast as he could, thankful to be off the streets and away from the Verzet—the Resistance.

For Tygo was in the unfortunate position of being both hunted and held captive. Hunted by the Resistance for collaboration with the Nazis; and held captive in service to Oberst Krüger, the chief of the "Sicherstellung" department of the SS in Amsterdam.

The Germans had such a department in every city they occupied. *Sicherstellung* meant "safekeeping," but the locals had another name for it. They called it the Plunder Squad, for that was what it was.

Since the Occupation the Nazis had taken it upon themselves to steal anything and everything of value. They had started with gold, jewelry, precious works of art—stripping the banks, museums, and then the fine houses until they were taking literally anything they wanted. And they had used Tygo's father, the best locksmith in all of Amsterdam, to help them do it. His father had complied rather than watch the Gestapo execute his family, until he was himself shot as a collaborator by the Resistance almost a year ago.

And so it had become Tygo's turn to be Krüger's locksmith, and dodge the ever-watching, ever-waiting Verzet.

Either way he knew he was damned.

He kept up his pace along the ice. The wind was easing a little, and he felt sweat running down his spine beneath the almost comical layers of clothing he was wearing: overcoat, jacket, sweater, shirt, vest. He was getting close to Euterpestraat, where the Gestapo had their headquarters and Krüger his comfortable, warm office on the third floor. He would get as close as he could on the ice, then run the last few hundred yards to the building.

Tygo's stomach rumbled. He hadn't eaten anything the day before except for some tulip-bulb soup from a soup kitchen, and that wasn't even food, really. There was no food now, or light or gas or electricity, for anyone except the occupying Germans. At least the exercise was keeping him warm, he thought.

He wondered briefly what Krüger would make him do that day. It had been quiet since the New Year and Tygo had been sent home most mornings after reporting in. Well, not home exactly. He no longer stayed there, not since the incident on Christmas Day.

He'd been asleep upstairs in the back bedroom above the shop. Unlike the previous Christmas, when they were still a family and there had been a little food, a few bits of coal for the fire, and even a few paltry gifts to give to his parents and his sister, Tygo had been alone in the house, curled up under a heap of damp, fetid blankets, trying to keep warm.

Luckily, he had taken the precaution of setting a metal bucket filled with rubble on top of the door at the top of the stairs.

A startled yell and the sound of someone falling had woken him. He had leapt from his bed and jumped out the back window into the yard below, where he had left a rope secured to the high brick wall. He had sprained his ankle in the jump, but just managed to scale the wall and drag the rope over the other side before the Resistance fighters had burst out through the back door.

He had crept back the following day under cover of darkness and retrieved his tools, which he now stored at Gestapo HQ, but since then he had slept at a different location every night: empty basements, church crypts, always on the move.

"You can run, but you can't hide!" one of the Resistance men had yelled after him.

Well, he'd keep running and just hope they'd never catch him.

Tygo turned off the main canal and followed the narrower Nordcanal to the point closest to Euterpestraat. He skidded to a halt on the ice, the skates making a satisfying screech, then climbed the stone steps from the landing jetty and sat down at the top to unlace his skates. They were beautiful: practically unused, black leather uppers with strong white laces looped through brass eyelets and shiny silver blades with sharp serrated edges at the toes. Tygo was ashamed to admit he had found them in a house he had been searching with Krüger on New Year's Day and had asked Krüger if he could have them.

"If you like." Krüger had shrugged. "But remember—you are only looking after them till the owners return."

Tygo knew he was just joking. The house had had a large yellow star painted on the front door, and everyone suspected that the Jews of Amsterdam would never return.

Tygo knotted the tops of the laces together and swung them over his shoulder. He pulled on his own boots, shabby and worn, that had been slung around his neck. Then he stood up and cautiously looked around. The coast appeared to be clear and he set off at a slow jog, the sidewalks too treacherous to allow a faster pace.

He was just passing an alleyway when a four-wheeled wooden cart, the sort used for foraging by one and all, shot out and caught the backs of his knees, pitching him forward onto the street. Before he could roll over, the owner of the cart had jumped on his back and jammed something cold and hard behind his right ear.

"Don't move a muscle!" It was a girl's voice. "We've got you this time, Winter."

Tygo tried to turn his head to see his assailant, but she prodded the muzzle of the pistol harder into the soft part of his neck at the base of his earlobe. It hurt.

"What do you want?" he asked, but he knew the answer. Was he about to meet the same fate as his father? He felt his stomach churn.

"Shut up and do exactly as I tell you!" He felt the weight of the girl's body lifting off him. "Stand up."

Tygo climbed to his feet, his heart pounding in his chest.

"Turn around."

He slowly turned to face his assassin in the murky light. Like him, she was bundled up against the cold, a fur hat with flaps crammed on her head, a scarf covering her face like a bandit's. She held an old-looking revolver in her woolen-gloved hand.

"Remember me?" she said.

Tygo stared at her, and after a moment she pulled the scarf from her face.

"Ursula? Ursula Kugler?"

They had been in the same class at the beginning of the war. She had been a pretty girl with lots of freckles, who always wore her hair in pigtails. He remembered her flicking ink bombs at him, made from pieces of blotting paper. She didn't look pretty anymore, just cold and starving and mean.

"Look, just let me go."

Ursula laughed, a short, hard sound. "Are you joking? There's a price on your head, and you're mine."

Tygo looked around. If he made a run for it, would she really shoot? He doubted it—but just then, as if reading his mind, Ursula cocked the revolver and raised it, outstretched, so that it was pointing at his heart.

"Step into the alleyway, stand against the wall, and put your hands behind your back." She kept her distance as Tygo did as he was ordered.

"Come on, Ursula, we used to like each other." He remembered how he would catch her looking at him in geography.

"Like *you*? A stinking collaborator? Let me see your hands!"

Tygo glanced back; she now had a length of rope in one hand and the revolver in the other.

"I don't have a choice, Ursula, you know that."

"We all have a choice; you made yours and I made mine. I hope they string you up with this rope from the nearest lamppost." That was now the most common form of execution for collaborators; bullets had become too precious to waste on them.

Tygo felt her edging closer to him. He tried to control his breathing, felt every muscle in his body tense.

"Put your hands together, on top of each other . . ."

Tygo pivoted fast, spinning to face her. So fast that the skates flew off his shoulders and the blade of one hit Ursula square across the bridge of the nose. She fell back onto the ground, blood pouring from the deep cut the skate had opened, and lay on the cobblestones, groaning with pain.

She had dropped the gun in the fall. It was a couple of feet away. They both saw it at the same time but she was faster, managing to grab ahold of it and bring it up to bear on Tygo.

Tygo leapt forward and landed on top of her, both his hands wrapping around her wrist. He slammed her hand down onto the cobbles—once, twice, three times—and the gun fell. She was crying, the blood blinding her now.

Tygo's heart was hammering, a terrible rage filling his head. He grabbed the skates and jammed one of the blades against the girl's neck. Her face was crimson, so much blood . . .

"I hate you, Tygo," she spat.

Tygo pressed the blade down harder. "I hate you too."

Ursula suddenly jammed her knee up as hard as she could. Tygo felt an intense, agonizing pain flood his groin; he cried out and rolled off her. Ursula was on her knees searching for the gun, desperately mopping the blood from her eyes with her scarf. Tygo gritted his teeth against the pain, on his knees now too. He swung at Ursula, but she blocked the blow with her forearm. He swung again, and for a moment he thought they must look like two dwarfs boxing in the alleyway. Finally one of his punches struck the girl's chin full force, and she went down and stayed down.

Tygo pulled himself to his feet, retrieved his skates and the revolver, and left his old classmate lying where she fell.

He jogged the rest of the way up Euterpestraat, the knuckles on his right hand red and swollen, stopping only to stash the gun and skates in a street culvert he used as a hiding place, close to the Gestapo headquarters.

He sat down for a minute or two on the snow-covered pavement and gazed up at the imposing redbrick building with its clock tower, at the windows draped with Nazi banners. The entrance was heavily sandbagged and bristling with armed guards. The next day he would have to use another route to get here. He didn't want to run into Ursula again, that was for sure.

His heart slowed, and suddenly he felt close to tears. That stupid girl had made him do it, made him hurt her. Why couldn't she just have let him go? Why couldn't all of them just leave him alone?

He got up and brushed the snow from his coat. It was all so unfair. But as Krüger liked to remind him: In the world they now inhabited, nothing was fair.

3

Just after ten Oberst Krüger emerged from his office. He had been meeting with a local man, Han van Meegeren, an influential artist and dealer in the city. He was reputed to have sold several Vermeers to Hermann Goering, the head of the Luftwaffe, for millions of guilders. Tygo was pretty sure the Oberst used him as a source of information for the whereabouts of hidden loot.

The two men parted company in the corridor with smiles and handshakes before Krüger turned his attention to Tygo. "Don't just sit there, Frettchen, we have work to do!"

Tygo jumped up from the hard chair opposite Krüger's office door where he always waited. Today he had a small plug of potter's clay in his pocket to pass the time.

"Frettchen" was the nickname Krüger had given Tygo soon after he had conscripted his services. It was German for "ferret." Krüger thought it suited him perfectly: Like the animal, he was used to seek out treasure for his master. It also suited him physically, he said, with his thin lanky body, shock of black hair, and dark brown eyes. Watchful, always alert. The name had stuck, and now everyone in Headquarters called him by it. Tygo had grown used to it and had decided to think of it as a badge of honor. Ferrets were born survivors, he told himself, and they had very, very sharp teeth.

Tygo followed Krüger back into his office and watched as he slipped his black leather Gestapo greatcoat off its hanger on the coat stand, put it on, and buttoned it up. He was fastidious about his appearance: his nails were always manicured, his hair slicked down with pomade, a straight part down the middle, the sides clipped close. He crossed to his desk and opened the top drawer, extracting a black leather belt with a holster attached. He strapped that on over the coat, checked that the pistol was loaded, and slid it back into the holster. It was a Sauer 38H, hammerless. Krüger preferred it to the Walther PPK that was standard issue for the Gestapo: You could carry it in your trouser pocket, he said, without the risk of snagging the hammer and shooting yourself in the foot.

Behind him was a large safe with the door still open. Tygo edged closer, trying to see inside. He had found plenty of plunder in the time he had been working here, and he was pretty sure the Oberst had failed to pass it along to Berlin. Krüger kicked the door shut with the heel of his boot before Tygo could catch a glimpse.

"No peeking, Frettchen." He turned the handle and twisted the key. It was attached to a little leather key case, which he snapped shut and put, as he always did, in his left trouser pocket. He glanced at himself in the mirror above the fireplace, tilting his black cap with its death's-head badge to a slightly rakish angle. Satisfied with his appearance, he marched out of the office.

Tygo followed.

They drove south, out of the city. Out into the suburbs where the canals were longer and straighter, the houses grander. Even here, though, the poplars and lime trees that once lined the streets had been cut down for timber and fuel. Nothing moved, the ground was frozen solid—and so, it seemed, were the people who were almost motionless on the streets, like statues.

Krüger stared out the window, a steady beat of anticipation in his chest. Six months he had been looking, searching this city for the stone: the fabled Red Queen diamond, which had been the centerpiece of the Russian Imperial Royal Crown. And today—finally—with the help of van Meegeren's new information, he was sure he was going to find it.

It was the mission General Müller had sent him to Amsterdam to carry out six months ago. A mission he knew he must not fail. Müller had never explained the significance of the stone, or why it was important, just that it must be recovered at all costs.

Up till now every lead, every tip-off had come to nothing. Still, the previous six months had not been without reward. Except for one unfortunate occasion, the young man beside him had been most compliant in helping Krüger amass a very healthy haul of valuables. His safe back at HQ was stuffed with gold, diamonds, and other stones, as well as stock certificates and bonds, all discreetly kept off official records.

Now, so long as he could finish Müller's job, he was in a position to put his own plan into action. He was a good Nazi but an even better survivor, and any fool could see the war was lost. It was time to get out, get away before it was too late.

When the time came—and he was pretty sure it would be soon—he would shed his black caterpillar body with its lightning-bolt runes and, with his stolen loot and the right documents, complete his metamorphosis into a South American butterfly. It was an extraordinary but true fact that the caterpillar and the butterfly were two completely different creatures, bearing no relationship to each other whatsoever. That would be him, Krüger thought.

But first the Red Queen had to be recovered.

He glanced over at the boy, sullen beside him. Since the incident back in September when Krüger had had to take a firm hand with him, he had lost his youthful arrogance, become withdrawn, watchful, scared even.

"Cheer up, Frettchen," he said, "you're still alive. The Resistance haven't got you yet."

"Yes, Herr Oberst, I'm sorry."

"That's more like it. We must all make hay while the sun shines."

He knew Tygo couldn't tell if he was teasing him. Krüger liked that.

The car slowed at a crossing. Two bodies were swinging from ropes strung around street lamps. Collaborators or Resistance fighters, it was hard to tell—he couldn't read the crude inscriptions on the cards tied to their coats.

Krüger looked back at Tygo. "What do you hope for the New Year, Frettchen?"

Probably just to survive, he thought. The boy's mother and father were gone, his sister far away or dead too; there was nothing left for him to think or care about except the need to stay alive. Tygo hesitated.

"Come along, Frettchen, indulge me. What do you hope for?"

"That I may serve you and the Führer until final victory is won for the Reich over all its enemies."

Krüger hooted with laughter. "Good answer, Frettchen, you're a wily little devil. Nothing would give you greater pleasure than sticking a knife in my back, don't think I don't know it."

"Herr Oberst, I assure you—"

"And I wouldn't blame you, but remember this: Continue to help me and there is a possibility I will save you; try anything stupid and I will cut you down where you stand. *Verstehst du?*"

"Yes, Herr Oberst."

They were driving slowly down an elegant avenue lined with tall poplar trees. Large villas were set back from the road behind thick hedges.

"Günter, stop at the next house on the right," Krüger instructed the driver. "Wait here unless I call for you. And keep your eyes peeled and your gun with the safety off. I wouldn't put it past the Resistance to be lurking—especially if they knew Frettchen here was around."

Tygo waded through the deep snow behind Krüger up the driveway toward the large Italianate villa. The place was clearly empty, the shutters closed, with no tracks in the snow leading up to the imposing front door. Tygo looked up at the house. The rain gutter along the roof had broken and an enormous icicle had grown down from it till it almost reached the portico above the doorway. For some inexplicable reason he felt a cold shudder run down his spine. A sense almost of foreboding, but then, he thought, abandoned old buildings always did seem sinister.

The front door had been padlocked shut and a sign posted across it: PROPERTY OF THE THIRD REICH. ENTRY STRICTLY FORBIDDEN, BY ORDER.

"Why are we here if it has already been searched?" Tygo said.

Krüger pulled off his black mohair-lined calfskin gloves and flicked the top of Tygo's freezing earlobe with his forefinger. It stung like hell. Tygo yelped.

"Since when did you ask the questions, Frettchen?" he snapped. "That is the preserve of the Gestapo. Now you do your job and I'll do mine. Open it up."

Tygo set the small leather case he was carrying down on the icy stone porch and took out a canvas roll. He spread it out on the ground, revealing a long line of lock picks. Glancing at the padlock briefly, he selected a tension bar to hold the locking bolt steady while he worked on the levers with the hook pick he selected. It was easy stuff for him, and he had it open in less than a minute.

"Very good, Frettchen. I see the cold has not affected your nimble little fingers."

Tygo drew back and Krüger turned the handle. The front door swung open silently, oil still on the hinges. Krüger drew his gun from its holster and stepped into the building, Tygo close behind.

They stood in the gloom for a moment in the large hallway. The place had been stripped of everything except the marble floor tiles they were standing on. A grand staircase wound its way up the side of the wall to a half-landing before continuing on to the first floor. On the walls were outlines where pictures or portraits had hung. It was deathly quiet.

Krüger turned on his heel and walked out of the hallway into a large room to the left. Shafts of winter light came in through chinks in the shutters, and Tygo could make out that it had been a grand reception room, oak-paneled all the way around, with a large fireplace surrounded by a carved wooden mantelpiece. Floor-to-ceiling French windows looked out to the grounds at the front. This room, too, had been cleared of all furniture. Tygo wanted to ask whose house it had been, but he didn't fancy another flick to the ear.

"Get the shutters open."

Tygo did as he was told, and light filled the room.

"We are looking for a small box, or a leather or velvet pouch, that has been hidden here," Krüger said. "Most probably in a wall or floor safe, or so my source believes. A safe that my colleagues missed when they took the house's other assets into safekeeping."

Tygo instinctively knew it was a piece of jewelry they were hunting. It must be worth a pretty penny for Krüger to be so intent.

Krüger clapped his hands. "*Macht schnell*, and let's get this done."

4

It took Tygo nearly until noon before he located the safe. He had had to explore the paneling minutely, but finally he had found a piece of beading that moved under his touch. Not loosely, but as though it had been planed and machined that way.

As he slid it to one side, the panel above rolled back, revealing a Milner's eight-lever mortise safe, probably installed when the house was built at the turn of the century. It was cemented securely into the thick brick wall. Tygo knew he had his work cut out—these were superb safes and well above his skills as a lock-picker. It would have taken his father a good couple of hours to get this one open, he thought. Nevertheless, with Krüger standing behind him, he had no choice but to try.

"Well? What are you waiting for?"

"It's a tough safe, sir."

"So? You're my expert. Get cracking."

Tygo nodded and considered how best to start. Some Milners had all sorts of anti-tamper devices, such as relocking pins that operated just when you thought you had successfully picked the levers. He worked hard for a good half hour as Krüger paced the room, smoking. But then his second hook pin snapped and he knew it was hopeless.

"I'm sorry, Oberst, I cannot continue."

"I don't know why I even bother with you," Krüger snapped. "Very well—we shall have to use a less subtle approach, and you had better hope that we do not damage the contents."

He marched out, returning a few minutes later with a small piece of green Plasticine-like substance in his hand. "Plastic explosive, Nobel 808," he said in response to Tygo's unasked question. "The British drop it for the Resistance. Very effective, so I am told."

Tygo watched as Krüger knelt down and rolled the explosive on the wooden floor like a piece of dough until he had fashioned a strip. He pressed this into the seam of the hinge side of the safe. Then he inserted a silver detonator rod into the soft explosive, to which he attached the exposed copper ends of some two-ply electrical wire. He picked up the roll of wire and began to spool it back toward the front door.

"Out!"

Tygo followed him into the hallway and out through the front door. Krüger had a detonator box waiting by the side of the porch. He cut the wire and quickly attached the copper contacts to the box. Tygo could see he was deft at this sort of thing and wondered briefly where he'd learned the skills. Krüger had never spoken to him about what he had done before he came to Amsterdam.

Krüger glanced up at Tygo. "Cover your ears and open your mouth."

Tygo did as he was told and Krüger dropped the plunger.

As the explosive went off, Tygo felt a massive thud in his chest from the shock wave. The whole house seemed to shake, and the windows exploded outward, tearing the wooden outdoor shutters from the walls.

"That should do the trick," remarked Krüger.

The two of them walked back into the room. It was wreathed in smoke, and there was glass all over the floor, which crunched underfoot. But the Nobel 808 had done its job. The heavy steel door had been blown clean off the front of the safe and was embedded in the wall opposite, still smoking.

Tygo grinned despite himself at the sight of it. Krüger was already at the open safe, thrusting his hand inside, but Tygo could see quite plainly that the baize-covered shelves were empty.

Krüger swore heavily, placed his hands on his hips, and looked around the wrecked room.

"It's got to be here. It's got to be!"

As he spoke, a heavy clump of soot dropped down the chimney and landed on the stone hearth. Krüger stared at it, and Tygo waited. He was clearly thinking something over.

"We haven't looked up there, Frettchen," he said.

"But, sir, that was just the explosion; it's shaken some of the soot free."

"Maybe, maybe not. So get up there and find out for sure."

Tygo walked across to the big fireplace. Stooping down, he ducked under the mantelpiece and flashed his flashlight up the narrow vertical passage. The chimney did not go straight up, but kinked to the right, not uncommon in such a large house.

Tygo knew he had no choice but to climb. Since he had worked for Krüger he'd been forced into every nook, cranny, and crevice in the old houses of Amsterdam. He had swum in flooded basements, crawled into hidden priest holes, found secret rooms—some even had families living in them.

The soot continued to fall as he made his way up the chimney, his legs braced on either side of the wall. He had wrapped a rag around his mouth to stop himself coughing. As he went higher, the chimney began to narrow and he found he could climb a little faster.

"Well, Frettchen?" Krüger called up.

"Nothing yet," replied Tygo. He reached up with his hand, and instead of brickwork, he found a ledge. He pushed with his legs, and his head and shoulders cleared the top of it. In the gloom he imagined the chimney opened out into some sort of void, about the height and width of a coffin. Tygo leaned forward into it with his legs pressed on the chimney wall behind him. He pulled the flashlight from his trouser pocket and flicked it on.

Two of the iciest blue eyes he had ever seen stared back at him out of a soot-blackened face. A girl.

The cold, hard shock of it stopped his heart for a second. Then his body instinctively jerked back, and before a scream of surprise could form in his throat he was tumbling back down the chimney.

He landed with a heavy thump on the stone hearth and lay there, winded, his elbows skinned. A fresh shower of soot shot down on top of him.

"Well, what is it?"

Tygo's mind was racing. In that split second he had seen both fear and desperation in those eyes—it was like staring at a helpless animal caught in a trap. He felt like that every morning when he woke, and every time he ventured out alone.

The words came out instinctively: "Nothing, sir."

"Nothing? Then why did you just fall down the chimney?"

Again, Tygo said the first thing that popped into his head. "There's a dirty great crow up there in a nest. It flew into my face." He pulled himself to his feet. "See for yourself if you don't believe me."

Krüger stared at him for a moment. "Well, it would seem we are too late on this particular occasion." He glanced around the room a final time, his expression one of disappointment mixed with frustration. "There is nothing more to be had from this place."

He marched out of the room and Tygo shook the soot from his hair. *That's where you're wrong*, he thought, glancing up the chimney. But there was only darkness and silence.

5

They returned to Euterpestraat in silence. Krüger was obviously brooding about his failure to find the wretched jewel, and Tygo was lost in thought about his extraordinary discovery and what he should do about it.

Günter drove past the entrance toward the rear of the building and down a ramp into the basement where the Gestapo kept their vehicles safe from the winter weather and sabotage. A car bomb had been used recently to kill a local party leader.

Krüger marched up the steel stairs till they reached ground level. He turned to give Tygo the once-over.

"Go and clean yourself up, for God's sake, and throw those clothes away. You're no good to me looking like a sweep. Ask the quartermaster for some fresh clothes on my authority."

Tygo nodded, miserable on the one hand to be once more inside this hateful place, but happy at the prospect of a shower and fresh clothes. The place was blissfully warm too.

The water hit him like sharp hot needles, and he stood under the shower for a good five minutes. It was nicest thing to have happened to him since the last shower he'd had. Then he picked up a block of shriveled soap that reeked of coal tar, and a scrubbing brush, and set to work. He watched the brown water swirling down the drain and smiled even though his skin was burning from the scrubbing. He was actually clean, for the first time in six weeks, the ingrained grime finally gone, the black around his fingernails banished. It felt glorious. He stepped out of the shower, wrapped a rough dry towel around his skinny waist, and walked across to survey himself quickly in the mirrors above the washbasins.

His ribs were sticking out and his elbows were skinned raw, but his skin was a blotchy clean pink that was wonderful to his eyes. He touched the raw skin and winced, then slowly got dressed. The quartermaster had provided him with a smaller version of the local police uniform—fresh socks, underpants, a warm woolen shirt, and strong-looking gray trousers and tunic.

Tygo took the comb out of the glass of disinfectant by the basin taps and ran it through his long hair, slicking it back. His dark eyes stared back at him, and despite himself he smiled. Whatever else might be happening, at least he felt human again, unlike that poor girl hiding in the chimney. He hadn't really stopped thinking about her since he'd gotten back, his mind returning every few minutes to those frightened, ice-blue eyes.

Hurrying up the stairs to the ground floor, he started to turn over a plan in his mind, but his thoughts disappeared as he reached the top. Two Gestapo officers were half carrying, half dragging a suspect down to the cells below. He looked young, not much older than Tygo, with a little Van Dyck mustache and beard, which were covered in crimson. His right eye was squeezed shut and a nasty purplish blue.

For an instant Tygo pictured himself crossing to the young man, punching the two guards out with lightning blows, and dragging him down the stairs, saying, "It's all right, I know a secret exit, we can get away!" For a moment he fantasized he was that boy of action, then he glanced away, ashamed, and hurried past them. If he had even tried to do something like that he would be cut down before he'd gone ten paces.

God, how he hated it all, this feeling of being trapped, with no way out other than a bullet from either the Nazis or the Resistance.

When he reached the third floor it was deathly silent. The staff had left for the day, and there was only a light on in Krüger's office at the far end of the corridor.

He walked along the linoleum-lined floor and stopped outside a door. Painted on it were the words: RECORDS DEPARTMENT.

31

Tygo stood there thinking for a moment or two, then looked around. The plan that was forming in his mind took another step forward. Here was an opportunity to find out about the house and its occupants . . . maybe even who the girl was, and a clue as to what exactly Krüger had been hunting for there. It was risky if he was caught, but the place was empty after all, and he would be quick about it.

He checked the corridor again and carefully turned the handle on the door. It was unlocked. He stepped inside.

"What are you doing?"

Tygo froze. He slowly turned and found a middle-aged, hatchet-faced woman standing behind the door, buttoning her woolen overcoat. She had already turned off all the lights as she prepared to leave, he realized.

She walked around Tygo and switched the lights back on. "Who are you?" She looked him up and down.

Tygo decided his only chance was to brazen it out. "I'm Tygo Winter. I assist Oberst Krüger in asset protection."

At the mention of Krüger's name, the woman's demeanor seemed to shift. Nobody, Dutch or German, wanted to cross Krüger.

"Well, what does the Oberst want?"

"Some information on a property on Voorthuizenstraat, number 73."

"Can't it wait till the morning?"

"No," said Tygo, taking a chance, "it's most urgent he has the information tonight."

The woman looked at Tygo, then marched between the ranks of filing cabinets until she stopped by one, opened the second drawer, ran her finger along the files inside, and eventually selected one. "Here you are—put it back when you have finished and close the door."

"Thank you, Miss . . ."

"It's Mrs.," the woman barked, and Tygo jumped.

He opened the file as she headed for the door. It was very thin. A map of the street with the property outlined in red and a note pinned to it: *This property is hereby transferred by the owner, the Bank of Utrecht, to the German authorities.* There was an official stamp issued by the Gestapo with the date December 7, 1940. Just over four years ago.

"Oh, Mrs. . . ."

The woman had the door open. "What? Be quick."

"It says the house was owned by the Bank of Utrecht. Can I get some information on that?"

"You'll be lucky—it was a private bank, owned by the Löwenstein family. They got out when the Nazis arrived—went to live in New York, I believe."

"Thank you. I'll tell the Oberst you have been most helpful."

"I'd rather you didn't," she said firmly, and left.

———————

"You took your sweet time, didn't you?" Krüger glanced up at Tygo from behind his desk. He held a lit cigarette in one hand and a glass of colorless liquid in a brandy balloon in the other. It was probably schnapps; that was what Krüger enjoyed. He claimed his grandfather used to make it from pears. The best, he said.

Tygo could tell he was irritated and annoyed. Whatever he had hoped to find in the house must have been important. Tygo suddenly realized something: On previous occasions when they had also come away empty-handed, Krüger had been in a similarly foul mood. Could it be that he had been searching for the same thing all this time?

"Sorry, Herr Oberst."

"Well, at least you look and smell a good deal better than you did."

Krüger got up and walked across to a small side table that held decanters and glasses. He refilled his glass, then, after a moment, dropped an inch of the liquid into a tumbler for Tygo. He handed him the glass.

"*Prost,*" he said, and banged his glass against Tygo's.

Tygo sipped the fiery liquid reluctantly.

"Don't sip it, boy!" Krüger said. "Down in one like a man."

Tygo threw it back into his throat and swallowed. He felt a pain behind the bridge of his nose, like when he ate a piece of ice. "Are you celebrating something, Herr Oberst?" he asked hoarsely.

"More like commiserating, Frettchen. Today was a great disappointment—I was hoping to find something . . . I have been searching for it for some time now." So Tygo's suspicion was correct after all. "Something that would be most helpful."

"Helpful?"

"To my future." Krüger smiled; the liqueur had lifted his mood temporarily. He refilled Tygo's glass over his objections and topped up his own. "That's it, let's drink to the future. God knows it's going to arrive very soon, and with a vengeance." He tossed back his drink, and Tygo did the same. He was already beginning to feel a tiny bit light-headed.

"What do you mean, sir?" asked Tygo.

"The head of the Gestapo, General Müller, is arriving here tomorrow to meet with me. To discuss a top-secret operation that is to be carried out in the next few days. What do you think of that, Frettchen?"

Tygo looked back at him and shrugged. Actually, he thought it sounded pretty scary—and pretty odd that Krüger was telling him about it.

"Why am I telling you, you may wonder, such a secret?"

Tygo nodded. He was wondering exactly that, and getting a bad feeling inside. Too much knowledge, as his history teacher used to say, was a dangerous thing.

"How long have you worked for me?"

"Six months," said Tygo.

"Six months . . . and we've gotten along pretty well, wouldn't you say?"

Tygo nodded again.

"There was that unfortunate business with your sister, but I think you learned your lesson from that."

Tygo nodded a third time. The mention of his sister took him instantly back to that terrible day last September when it had seemed liberation was at hand. The city was in turmoil, and he had refused Krüger's order to help him secure the central warehouses. He had paid a terrible price for his insubordination: As punishment Krüger had ordered his sister, the last remaining member of his family, to join the next train of "guest workers" going to Germany. It was the last he had seen of her, or was likely to.

"Learned that we need to trust each other?"

"Yes, sir."

"We *can* trust each other, can't we?" Krüger was looking carefully at him now as he repeated the question.

"Of course, Herr Oberst." Tygo hoped he sounded sincere. He didn't trust Krüger with the money for a pack of gum, and he never would.

"Good, Frettchen. A great many things may need to be arranged. Arranged in total secrecy and with great speed. That is why I have told you about this matter."

"I understand, sir." In truth, Tygo didn't have the faintest idea what all this was about.

"You will base yourself here at Headquarters until further notice. I will arrange some sleeping quarters for you."

The proposal both appealed to him and appalled him in equal measure. It meant his nights would at least be safe from the Resistance, but the thought of living in such a hellish place, where torture and murder were carried out every day, made him feel sick. There was no way he would ever live this down when the war did end—if he was lucky enough to survive, that was.

Krüger walked back to his desk and picked something up from it. "You are to carry this at all times."

It was a small brass disk with the Gestapo badge on one side, identifying the owner as a member of the Gestapo. Tygo slipped the badge into his pocket.

"And a letter, signed by myself, stating that you are acting on my authority and are to be given free passage throughout the Netherlands."

Tygo took the small envelope that Krüger handed him. He felt scared; such papers, if found on him by the Resistance, would certainly seal his fate. But then a spark of optimism struck him too. If you looked at it another way, they were a ticket to get away. He could move freely around the city—even the country—without being questioned. What other Dutch person could do that? For a moment it made him feel light-headed, giddy, but then he remembered the schnapps was probably the cause of that.

"If I help you, Herr Oberst, is there a chance my sister could be sent for?"

Krüger looked back at him. "I like you, Tygo, I like the fact that you're always ready to push your luck. I'm the same: Push your luck; only then will you find how far it goes. Well, unfortunately this is where it stops. Your sister is no longer a concern of mine; her fate has been sealed, by yourself if you recall. Better to forget she ever existed. Do we understand each other?"

Tygo nodded, hatred burning in his heart. He understood, all right. He would do everything that Krüger asked of him, and then he would use the letter and tag to escape this wretched city before it was too late. For the first time in a very long time, Tygo realized, he was thinking about something more than just day-to-day survival: He was thinking about the future.

6

Tygo was dog-tired but couldn't sleep. The room he had been given to sleep in was a broom cupboard in the basement, his bed a stained old mattress and an army blanket. Better than he had had for weeks, and he should have been fast asleep as soon as his eyes closed, but he wasn't. He lay there thinking about the house they had visited. And the girl. And the jewel that Krüger was looking for. Maybe Tygo could find it—or better yet, maybe the girl knew where it was—maybe she had it!

Tygo wondered if he should go back the next day to see what he could find. Then he felt the warrant disk in his pocket, next to the letter from Krüger. It meant he could break the nightly curfew if he wanted. What if he went now? It was after midnight, the streets would be deserted; it would be safer to travel now, and he would be back in time for Krüger the following morning.

A long, agonized cry came from one of the cells. It seemed

to pierce Tygo's heart, and he shivered. *No time like the present*, he thought, and got to his feet in the darkness, his hand searching the wall for the light switch.

He found an unused bicycle in the motor pool and, having shown his pass to the sentry, pushed it up the ramp from beneath the building and onto the street.

The city was enveloped in darkness, and there was just enough light from the waning moon for Tygo to see his way and strike out for the south of the city: 73 Voorthuizenstraat. He thought he could make it in about twenty minutes. It was bitterly cold and the snow had formed a hard crust on the roads; he had to be careful on the corners, but he could still cycle.

He never saw the rope, or twine, or whatever it was that had been strung across the road in front of him, in the darkness. It took him at chest height and lifted him clean off his saddle, and he flew backward. He was too surprised to tense up, and as a result—luckily for him—he landed very softly in a heap on the crusted snow, his back and shoulders taking the impact, the back of his head just knocking lightly on the road. He lay there, winded, for a moment, trying to figure out what had just happened, but then strong hands took hold of him and were pulling him up off the street and hauling him toward the sidewalk.

"Let go of me," he protested feebly. He knew immediately he was in big trouble. Dressed in the local Dutch police uniform, he could expect no mercy from the Resistance.

"Shut up," a young man hissed in his ear. The other person bent one of his arms up behind his back and jerked it sharply. A searing pain shot into his brain; it felt like his shoulder would dislocate.

"Okay, okay," Tygo yelped. A flashlight beam suddenly snapped on right in his face and he had to close his eyes.

"Well, looks like we've hit the jackpot tonight." A girl's voice; Tygo recognized it.

"Ursula . . ."

"The one and only."

For a moment, Tygo glimpsed his captors—two boys about the same age as him, their faces gaunt and filthy. Ursula stood farther back in the shadows. She had a large bandage across the bridge of her nose. Then the light snapped off.

"I said, shut up." Another hard jerk, another bolt of pain. Little red dots danced in front of Tygo's eyes.

"Well, what about that, Winter?" said Ursula. "It's just like trams: You wait for days and then two come along at the same time."

"Who is he?" asked one of the boys.

"This is Tygo Winter," said Ursula. "Collaborator."

"Yeah?"

"Search him." Ursula seemed to be in charge. One of the youths let go and came around to face Tygo, patting his clothing quickly and expertly.

Tygo was thinking fast. Three against one; it was going to

41

be difficult, and the other boys were strong. But he was pretty sure they wouldn't kill him. Ursula wanted that bounty money.

"I'm going to enjoy watching them kill you, Winter." Ursula came close, cleared her throat, and spat in his face. Tygo felt the thick blob of mucus run down his cheek. Managing to lean forward, he spat back as hard as he could.

Ursula drove her fist into his stomach and he doubled up. One of the boys was still holding his arm tightly behind his back, saving him from falling to the ground.

"Is that your best shot?" Tygo panted.

Before Ursula could respond, a different answer was provided. Down the street came the sound of a heavy vehicle, and a powerful spotlight swung out in a wide arc, raking the sidewalk and houses with its beam.

Ursula swore. Tygo felt the boy's grip on his arm slacken, and took his chance. He spun around and head-butted him as hard as he could. The boy pitched backward, clutching his face and yelling in pain, and Tygo took off up the street toward the light.

"Split up, go!" he heard Ursula shout behind him.

Tygo could make out the vehicle; it was a four-wheeled, light-armored car with a turret sprouting a machine gun. A field police officer was standing in the turret, operating the light. Tygo put up his hands as it landed on him.

"Tygo Winter, attached to Oberst Krüger's department. I have authority to be out!" he shouted at the top of his voice. It would be too much to avoid a bullet from the Resistance only to get one from the Germans.

"Come forward, slowly, with your hands up!" the policeman shouted.

Tygo walked forward.

"Your papers and identity disk!"

"They're in my tunic!"

"Slowly then, with your right hand."

Tygo carefully took out the disk and letter as the policeman climbed out of the turret and dropped to the ground. He took the documents and examined them under his flashlight.

"What reason do you have to be out this late?"

Tygo knew he had no choice but to lie at this point, bluff his way out. The worst that could happen was that they would take him back to HQ and he would have to face Krüger.

"A special mission for Oberst Krüger—I am not at liberty to say—his strict orders."

The policeman looked back at Tygo skeptically. "What is a young man like you doing for Oberst Krüger at this time of night?"

"Perhaps you should ask him yourself?" Tygo's heart was hammering in his chest for the second time in as many minutes.

The policeman took another glance at the letter, then handed it and the warrant disk back to Tygo.

"Be careful, young man, the Resistance is active in this

sector." With that he climbed back into the armored car and thumped the turret with his fist.

Tygo waited for the car to pass. Its light picked out his bicycle lying on the ground; Tygo ran to it and quickly climbed on board. He pedaled as hard and as fast as he could, but it was okay—Ursula and her friends hadn't hung around.

Ten minutes later he was at the villa. He parked the bicycle a little way from the drive and stole as quietly as he could through the deeper snow to the front door. Getting back inside took just a few minutes with his skeleton keys.

His footsteps on the stone floor in the hallway sounded incredibly loud. He tried his flashlight, but it didn't work; it must have broken in the fall. Tygo swore. He stood there for a few minutes, letting his eyes get used to the darkness; the place still had a metallic smell of explosives.

"Hello, is anybody here?" he called out softly. Perhaps the girl had fled after they had left. The sweat from the cycle ride ran down his spine and he shivered. He'd been in lots of empty buildings, but at night, alone, they never failed to scare him.

He went into the oak-paneled room and stared up the chimney. There was no way he was climbing back up it.

"I saw you," he said. "Come down if you're there. I won't hurt you . . ."

But there was only darkness and silence. He turned and made his way out of the room, his boots crunching on the

44

broken glass as if it were gravel. If the girl really wasn't there, he could concentrate on looking for the jewel.

Tygo decided to try the next floor; perhaps there was another safe hidden in the floor or wall somewhere else in the building. He slowly walked up the long, winding flight of stairs; each step creaked a little louder than the last. Tygo held on to the banister. It was rickety, with lots of spindles missing. Just as he reached the top, he felt something racing toward his face, the air whiffling. He screamed but the pigeon's wing only kissed his cheek as the bird flashed past him. He nearly toppled backward, but managed to grab the rail just in time. The pigeon flapped down into the darkness below and out of one of the shattered windows.

"Easy, Tygo," he muttered to himself. For a moment he wondered if it had all been in his imagination, if there had been no girl earlier. He felt inside his jacket and found what he was looking for: a few loose matches purloined from Krüger's crystal striker that he kept on the mantelpiece in his office.

Tygo leaned down and struck one on the stone step. He straightened up to get his bearings, holding the match in front of him, and only just saw the broken stair spindle coming toward him.

Crack—he felt himself falling down the stairs, his head hitting something impossibly hard. Then there was nothing but that sick feeling of oblivion.

7

It was the sound of an enormous explosion that brought Tygo around. He became conscious of the end of it, the boom rolling like thunder through the city, the sound both hard and resonant.

He opened his eyes, half expecting to be lying in the ruins of the villa. Instead he was on the marble stone of the hallway, his overcoat balled up and stuck under his head for a pillow. A single candle was burning beside him, giving a small circle of light. It was enough for him to see a girl, aged maybe fourteen or fifteen, sitting cross-legged beside him, staring down at him.

She was dressed in a dirty woolen overcoat that hung open, a woolen sweater underneath with a large hole almost where her heart would be, and a rough tweed shirt poking through the hole. She had a pair of hobnailed boots on her feet, their soles peeling away from the uppers, and no socks.

So he had not imagined her after all.

Her face was scrubbed clean of the sooty blackness he remembered from when he had last seen her; only her eyes were the same. Topaz, the color of a July sky. Tygo noticed a tiny cleft in her chin. A gold locket was tied around her neck with a piece of ribbon.

Tygo looked into those eyes again. He tried to remember the fear he'd seen in them, but now they were hard and calculating and aimed directly at him.

"Who are you?"

He tried to sit up and realized he couldn't: His hands and feet had been tied with strips of torn cloth. The girl was taking no chances.

Tygo tried to think of something to say.

"Who are you?" the girl repeated.

"Untie me and I'll tell you," said Tygo.

The girl tossed something toward him. It was his Gestapo warrant disk.

"Gestapo." She spat the word at him, picked up the stair spindle, and hit him hard in the ribs.

Tygo cried out in pain and sat up straight. "No!" he yelled at her. "I'm not Gestapo; I'm the son of a locksmith. We have— had—a shop near the station. Winter's—do you know it?"

The girl shook her head. "You're lying. It was you who came here today. I recognize you. You blew up the house."

"I'm not lying. Yes, I was here, but that other man who you didn't see, *he's* Gestapo, not me. He forces me to work for him, to help find stuff—valuable property, like jewelry."

Tygo wondered if the word "jewelry" would make her react, but her face remained cold, emotionless.

"Forces you?" She sounded skeptical.

"Yes, I swear. If I don't do what he says, he'll kill me—shoot me."

"Even if what you say is true, why are you here now?"

"I saw you. I . . . wanted to come back to see if you were real."

The girl snorted with contempt. "Oh, spare me. He was looking for something here, wasn't he?"

Tygo nodded. "Yes, a stone, I think. He likes diamonds."

"*That's* why you came back. Admit it."

"Maybe, partly—okay, yes, I thought I'd come back and see if I could find it. If I can get it for him, I think he will let me escape from the city."

"Why do you want to escape?"

"Why do you think?" Tygo burst out. "It's obvious, isn't it? Everyone thinks I'm a collaborator. The Resistance have a price on my head. They're going to kill me as soon as they get ahold of me. I need to get away."

The girl looked at him. "Is that a lie?"

Tygo shook his head, which was still throbbing. He felt a little bit nauseous.

"Why would I make up something like that?" he said. "Please untie me. I'm not going to hurt you."

The girl pursed her lips. "Does this man know you are here?"

"No," said Tygo emphatically. "And he has no idea *you're* here, either—I didn't tell him I'd seen you, I promise." He had managed to sit up now with his bound hands in front of him.

"You came back to search yourself?" she asked.

"Yes, like I said." He stared at her. "I suppose a bit of me did want to see if you were real too, not a ghost or my imagination in the dark up that chimney. *Are* you real?"

She leaned forward and hit Tygo lightly on the head with the spindle. "Does that feel real?"

"Ow!" Tygo yelped. "All right, yes."

The girl was clearly assessing him, trying to make up her mind.

"Look, how about this?" he went on. "If you help me find whatever that Gestapo man is looking for, I can help you leave this place, get some food."

"What makes you think I want to leave?"

Tygo looked back at her, stumped. "Well, it's cold, it's lonely . . . and to be honest, for all I know, Krüger may come back here. Please untie me."

"Shut up, I'm thinking," the girl replied. She half closed her eyes; Tygo could see he might be getting through to her.

Whatever she might say, she was in the same boat as him: alone, hungry, scared, and cold. And that was just for starters.

"Let me help you," he ventured.

"I don't need your help—seems to me you need mine more." The girl crossed her arms defensively.

"Fine, then, go on living by yourself halfway up a chimney."

"I was only up there because of you! And anyway, who says I'm alone?"

Tygo shrugged. "Just a wild guess."

She remained silent.

"Look, think about it sensibly for one minute. We can help each other. And whatever you say, we both need help." Tygo felt a sudden welling-up of loneliness and loss inside him. An aching, burning feeling that rose up his throat. "Just untie me, please. I'll leave you alone, all right? I made a mistake."

His voice was hoarse, his eyes wet. The girl looked at him, then knelt forward and started to undo his bonds. "If you try anything funny . . ." she warned.

"I won't, I promise." Tygo rubbed his wrists where the cloth bindings had dug into his skin. "What is your name?" he asked.

"Willa," the girl replied.

"Willa?"

"Short for Wilhelmina."

"Wilhelmina Löwenstein, by any chance?" said Tygo.

The girl looked startled for a moment, then carefully

continued untying him. Tygo eased himself up to a sitting position. He felt a lump on the side of his head where he had hit the stone stairs. Fortunately the skin was unbroken.

"Did I . . . ?" He pointed to the stairs.

"All the way to the bottom. I was sure you were dead. What do you know about the Löwensteins?"

"Nothing—I mean, I just know who they were, and that they used to live here, a long time ago, before the war."

"They never lived here. My mother lived here with me—until a few weeks ago." Willa sounded almost bitter.

"I don't understand. The title document said the house was owned by a bank belonging to the Löwensteins."

Willa looked at Tygo. "How do you know that?"

"I looked it up last night, in the records department. The house was passed to the German authorities when they invaded. It was raided by Krüger's department, the Sicherstellung."

"I know, I was there!" The girl was angry at the memory. "They cleared the house of everything—we hid with friends and returned when they had sealed the place up. We've lived here secretly ever since."

"But if you're not Willa Löwenstein, who are you?"

Willa stared at Tygo, clearly trying to decide whether to trust him. Finally she spoke.

"My mother was Pieter Löwenstein's mistress; he kept this house for her. I am his child. When the Germans came he bought safe passage for himself and his wife and legitimate children. He left my mother and me here. My mother was a Catholic, but he is my father, so under the law of the Germans I am a Jew. And everyone knows what happens to them."

"Right," said Tygo. He didn't know what else to say. All the Jews in the country had long ago been rounded up and shipped away on trains to who knew where.

"My mother told me that my father had sworn he would arrange for us to follow him to New York, but she never heard from him again."

"Perhaps he tried?"

"Perhaps. Or perhaps we were an inconvenience."

Outside a clock struck and Tygo counted the strokes: six. Six a.m.—the night had flown by and, like Cinderella, he would have to be getting back to Headquarters soon. Krüger hated it if he was a minute late. He realized there was something he had not asked the girl.

"And where is your mother now?"

Willa turned away from him but he caught the sadness. Of course, how stupid of him. He didn't say the word—he didn't have to. It was obvious now. *Dead.* Just like his parents.

"How long ago . . . ?"

The girl leaned in to him and gave a sob, and without thinking Tygo pulled her close to him—not just to comfort her but to hide the tears in his own eyes. Tears that had sprung from hearing her story and the pain he suddenly felt inside for the loss of his own family.

"Christmas Eve," sobbed Willa. "It'd been snowing hard all day. She went to fetch some of the dry wood we'd hidden in the backyard before the snow became too deep. It was late in the evening; she wanted us to keep the fire in for Christmas morning as a treat. I must have fallen asleep. When I woke up, she wasn't there. I went outside . . . it was light, the snow was up to my waist. I found her lying underneath the bushes where we had hidden the wood. On her back, her eyes closed. So peaceful, I thought she was asleep. But she wasn't."

"I'm sorry," said Tygo.

Willa pulled away from him and wiped her eyes. "I think she knew she was dying—she gave me her locket on Christmas Eve. Usually she never took it off. She made me swear to keep it safe."

Tygo looked at her. She was just like him, all alone now, with a cold, hostile world outside waiting for them. "Come with me," he said impulsively. "Let me help you now."

"No, I can't. If I go out, I'll be arrested. I don't have papers or anything."

"I'm going to help you," said Tygo fiercely. And he really meant it.

"How can you possibly help me?" she said.

Tygo looked at her, thinking. "Well, I can come back later with some food and drink. Bread, soup, maybe even a little sausage . . ." Even to Tygo's ears it sounded incredible, a fantasy, but Willa just shrugged. "After that—well, I'll think of something, a way to get you out of here. If you stay here you're going to die, just like your mother."

"Why do you care?"

For a moment Tygo was flummoxed. Why *did* he care about this strange girl? Why didn't he just leave her? He wasn't entirely sure, but there was one very good practical reason.

"Because I need you."

"For what?"

"To help me find what Krüger's looking for. It could help us both."

Willa frowned. "We'll see" was all she said.

8

The first orange streaks of dawn flashed across the top of the flat, gray North Sea and met the tiger-striped S-boat racing toward the rising sun. The German attack boat was at full speed—over forty knots—anxious to be in position now it was light.

General Müller was inside the small bridge, holding on to the rail by the wheel, trying to stop the seasickness building up to a point of no return. He hated boats.

"Not long now, Herr General!" the captain called out to him from the other side of the wheel. He was scanning ahead with a pair of powerful binoculars. "There, about a half mile to port, the marker buoy."

The boat slewed to the right and raced toward the target, the hull banging down on the swell. Shortly thereafter, the big Mercedes engines throttled back and the S-boat started to slow. The captain spoke into the ship's intercom.

"This is your captain speaking, now hear this. We are in position. All engines stop. Action stations."

"Excellent work, Captain," Müller said quietly. "May I remind you that what you are about to witness is the greatest secret of the Reich. If you or your men breathe so much as a word about it—"

"I assure you, Herr General," the captain interrupted the threat that was coming, "I can vouch for every man on my ship."

The sun was above the horizon now. Müller and the captain made their way out of the bridge and onto the foredeck, next to the small anti-aircraft turret. Müller's nausea was now replaced with the flutter of anticipation.

"The moment of truth," he said to the captain. The rest of the crew were on deck, watching expectantly, even the engineers in their greasy overalls.

About thirty miles out from the Dutch coast, the S-boat rocked on the calm sea, nothing to be seen in any direction. They could have been on the surface of the moon. They waited.

There was no warning, no rumble, no sound, just a sudden plume of water exploding two hundred yards in front of them. A plume that instantly became a squat, black missile with a tongue of flame, white and blue at its base, blasting it skyward.

The two men watched it streak up into the dark-blue morning sky, the waning moon still visible above it. As it leapt higher it left a long white chalk line of vapor.

"*Mein Gott,*" the captain finally mustered.

"God had nothing to do with it," Müller replied.

What they had just witnessed changed everything, he thought. The war *could* be won, even now, even this late in the day. This was the evidence. The Führer had said if the sea trial was successful, then they would go. Operation Black Sun would be authorized.

The bow of the Type XXI U-boat burst through the surface from where the rocket had appeared, and the S-boat blasted its siren—*whoop whoop whoop*—in congratulation. Müller and the captain took off their hats and waved them in salute as the submarine settled on the surface.

Within less than a minute the conning tower was manned by the U-boat captain and his signaler, their Aldis lamp flashing Morse messages.

Müller and the captain returned to the bridge, where Müller took the transcript of the U-boat's message from the S-boat's signaler. It read: "*Test fire complete. All systems are green. Awaiting further orders.*"

"Signal to the U-boat commander as follows." Müller thought for a moment. "*The Führer will be notified of your superb achievement. You may now unseal your destination orders and proceed immediately to the rendezvous point. Heil Hitler.*"

The signaler hurried back to his lamp.

"And once he has done that, Captain," Müller added, "get us out of here before the RAF have us for breakfast!"

9

Tygo cycled back to Gestapo Headquarters through the frozen streets. It was bitterly cold; his nose ran and his cheeks burned. Ursula and her gang were nowhere to be seen; perhaps they were sitting in that alleyway from the day before, hoping to snare Tygo again.

About half a mile from Headquarters he discovered the cause of the explosion that had woken him back in the villa: A British Lancaster bomber had crashed. It must have been on its way to a raid, carrying its payload of a single twelve-ton blockbuster bomb, by the look of things.

It had certainly lived up to its name: An entire city block of houses had been demolished, leaving the ones opposite barely touched. There must have been twenty houses gone. The street was cordoned off and flames still danced up from a few of the buildings; there wasn't a fire department anymore. A few civilian defense workers were gingerly trying to pick through the rubble, looking for any possible signs of life.

Tygo stopped to stare for a few minutes. It was staggering to him that they could make weapons now of such incredible power. Imagine a whole street destroyed by a single bomb—it was just amazing. Goebbels, the Minister of Information, had spoken in a radio broadcast of a *Wunderwaffe*, a wonder weapon, which was a thousand times more powerful than these monster bombs and could destroy whole cities, but everyone knew that was just a propaganda lie. Such a weapon was impossible, unthinkable; all the explosives in the world couldn't do something like that.

Tygo stayed to watch a bit longer, then, conscious of the time, pressed on and arrived back at Headquarters before eight.

"Good morning," he said to the tired-looking guard who was checking his papers.

"What's so good about it?" the guard replied, handing him back the document and warrant disk.

"I don't know," said Tygo. But he did feel different—was it meeting Willa, or something else? He wasn't sure.

He sat on his usual hard chair outside Krüger's office in the corridor. The light was on inside and he could hear Krüger talking on the telephone. It was very early for him to be at work, Tygo thought. His stomach was rumbling badly, but it would be better to wait until Krüger had seen him than to slip off to the cafeteria now. He would have to find a way of smuggling some food out for Willa too, he reminded himself. He liked the feeling of thinking about someone else again.

The office door opened and Krüger strode out, buttoning his leather overcoat. He seemed preoccupied, distracted, barely glancing at Tygo.

"Come along, Frettchen." Curt, cold.

Tygo fell into step beside Krüger. A short car ride later, and they were outside 321 Keizersgracht, an elegant, classic-looking Amsterdam town house with a heavy wooden front door and a large brass knocker in the shape of a lion. Krüger's black-gloved hand struck the knocker twice. After a moment, the door opened and a middle-aged woman stood before them.

"Frau van Meegeren?"

"Yes," she said faintly, her face almost gray from fright at the vision of Krüger in his black uniform. She was blinking uncontrollably.

"Oberst Krüger, Geheime Staatspolizei. I would very much like to speak to your husband; is he here?" Krüger knew he was: The house had been under observation since the early hours.

The woman nodded and stepped back awkwardly. Krüger clicked his heels politely and stepped inside.

"Upstairs, in the salon," the woman said, waving weakly toward the staircase.

"Thank you, Frau van Meegeren."

Tygo followed Krüger up the gilded staircase. The walls were hung with Old Masters, and on the landing polished sculptures and vases rested on side tables. It was as if the war wasn't happening here. Certainly the place was cold, but there was an incredible smell too. Tygo tried to place it . . . bacon? Yes, the place smelled of bacon and coffee, or was it tobacco? It smelled wonderful, at any rate.

Krüger marched straight into the large second-floor salon. It too was richly furnished, with leather and velvet-covered furniture, and thick Persian carpets on the polished elm floors. A middle-aged man was kneeling down in front of the fireplace, a poker in his hand. He turned at the sound of their entrance. His eyes registered surprise, but not fear. Tygo immediately recognized him as the man who had visited Krüger's office the day before.

"Well . . . good morning, Oberst, please come in." Van Meegeren stood and reached for his pipe on the mantelpiece. "I have some fresh coffee if you would like?"

"Perhaps later. First we talk; time is very much of the essence."

Van Meegeren nodded. "I understand then that yesterday's search was unsuccessful?"

"You understand correctly."

Van Meegeren sat down in a large comfortable-looking chair. "I'm sorry," he said, but he didn't sound it.

Krüger sat opposite him.

"Would you care for some food?" Van Meegeren indicated a tray on a side table, which held a coffeepot and some delicious-looking cookies.

"No, I would not! This is not some tea party. I want answers, van Meegeren, or I will take you outside and shoot you in the street."

Tygo edged toward the table where the food was. He could see Krüger was deadly serious, and was glad he wasn't the focus of his anger. Van Meegeren appeared to wilt from this threat, his face flushing and his air of calm deserting him.

"Of course. Did you find the safe?"

"Empty."

"Then it must still be with Löwenstein's mistress."

"I have checked with our records department, with the local police. Everyone. There is no evidence this woman exists—no identity papers, nothing on the file."

"No evidence of her at the house?"

Krüger shook his head.

Tygo was by the table now. He glanced at the two men, but neither gave him a second look. Quickly he turned his back, folded up the linen napkin the cookies were sitting on, and popped it into his coat pocket.

"Wait a minute," van Meegeren suddenly exclaimed. "She had a daughter, a young girl."

At that Tygo spun around, and he knew van Meegeren had caught both the cookie theft and the look of surprise on his face. Tygo cursed himself inwardly.

"She was about nine or ten at the start of the war. Pretty girl, what was her name . . . ? Began with a W, I think."

Krüger was nodding. "We will check."

Tygo could see that the art dealer was watching him carefully. He felt his cheeks coloring. Van Meegeren began to smile, and not in a good way.

"Yes, check—the mother might have given her daughter the stone. Perhaps this young man can help you."

Krüger shot a look at Tygo.

"What do you mean?" Tygo protested.

"You know something." Van Meegeren's tone was mild, but Tygo felt his stomach turn over.

"I do not!" Tygo said firmly. "I don't know anything."

Van Meegeren shrugged. "I must be mistaken." He looked back at Krüger. "I will make some inquiries immediately, Oberst."

"Be sure that you do."

Krüger got to his feet, and Tygo followed him out of the room. He glanced back at the doorway; van Meegeren was still sitting in his chair. He tapped his index finger against his nose and Tygo hurried out, deeply uneasy.

———————

Tygo tried to avoid Krüger's glances on the way back to HQ. Thankfully, once there, the Oberst became focused on the imminent arrival of General Müller.

When Müller did arrive just after midday, Tygo was amazed to see he was unaccompanied by any other officers. He was carrying a black attaché case, and Tygo thought he exuded a menacing sort of power, like the evil witches in fairy tales who made flowers shrivel and die as they passed.

Krüger hurried out of his office and saluted him. "An honor, General."

Müller returned the salute and Krüger followed him inside. He flicked his hand at Tygo, indicating for him to get lost, then closed the door.

Tygo sat on his chair for a moment. The head of the Gestapo was sitting not five yards from him. Something out of the ordinary was happening, that was for sure. Tygo got to his feet; he didn't want to hang around, and Krüger would be busy with Müller for a while, so perhaps now would be an ideal time to go back to Willa. He had cookies after all.

He started down the corridor, then stopped. He knew he was taking a risk but he wanted very badly to know what on earth was going on. He tiptoed back to the door, gingerly putting his ear to the doorjamb. Müller was in midsentence.

"Herr Oberst, I am at a loss as to your failure; you have had six months to carry out the task I sent you here for. Where is this stone? Thousands of man-hours have been put into it to make sure every aspect of this operation is successful. It has more moving parts than the finest Swiss watch, and each one must work perfectly and precisely. One of those little pieces, one tiny cog . . . Yet all you have done, no doubt, is squirrel away some nuts for the winter for yourself!"

"Herr General, I can assure you I have been searching for the stone night and day, without let-up; in fact only yesterday I was positive—"

"The Red Queen is more than just a diamond. It is essential to the success of this mission. The Führer has given his word to the señorita."

"On the Führer's life, I will find the stone."

So that was what Krüger had been looking for all these months: a single stone. Tygo had been right.

"It must be in my hand in two days—by the *geheime Flug* on January fourteenth—or we won't be speaking of the Führer's life but of yours, Oberst Krüger."

"I understand, Herr General." Tygo thought he could detect a note of fear in Krüger's voice. It was not something he'd ever heard before.

"Very well, I will move on to the other elements of the operation. First, the contents of this briefcase . . ."

Tygo took this as his cue to hurry away down the corridor. *Geheime Flug* meant "secret flight." And what was the promise made by the Führer? Something huge was going on, but what did it all mean? Tygo promised himself he would find out.

10

Travel in daylight hours was relatively safe for Tygo, and after passing through a couple of checkpoints he made it back to the villa in good time. He unlocked the front door again, using his picks, and stepped inside.

"Willa?" he called out confidently. "It's me, Tygo. I've come back, like I said."

He waited in the hallway for her to respond. Nothing.

"Willa?" Tygo was suddenly worried that maybe she was gone. That maybe he would never see her again. For some reason that mattered to him.

"I've brought food for you . . ."

There was a creak of a board from behind, and Tygo spun around. Willa was standing a couple of yards from him, still armed with the stair spindle.

"Show me."

Tygo reached into his pocket and brought out the folded napkin. He opened it in the palm of his hand. "They're fresh-baked."

Willa stepped closer and looked at the cookies. "They're oatmeal?" she said, amazed. "Actual oatmeal?"

"Go on, have one—have them all."

Willa picked one up, sniffed it, then took a small bite. She chewed for a moment, then smiled at Tygo before stuffing the rest of the cookie into her mouth. Tygo grinned. He felt like he used to at Christmas when he handed his sister her gift.

"Sit down and enjoy them."

Tygo went to sit at the foot of the stairs and Willa joined him. He handed her the napkin and she started on her second cookie. She was clearly starving. Tygo watched her eat a second and then a third.

"Well, have you thought about it?"

"About what?" Willa started on the last cookie.

"That you help me find the jewel Krüger needs. I've found out something: It's a diamond called the Red Queen."

Willa shrugged. "I don't know anything about that."

Tygo stared at her. Was she telling the truth? He shrugged off his disappointment.

"Still," he said at last, "you might be able to help, and anyway, I don't think you should stay here. Krüger knows you exist."

"How?" Willa looked alarmed now. "You told him, didn't you? You snitched on me!" Her alarm was turning to anger.

"No, I swear, I would never do that. He went to see a man who told him about you and your mother."

Willa leapt to her feet. "I wish I'd never met you."

"I can hide you, it's all right."

"How? How will we get across the city? I have no papers."

Tygo grabbed ahold of her arm, but she shook him off.

"I have my warrant disk and letter of authority," he said. "I can tell the checkpoints I'm taking you in on Krüger's authority."

"And that's exactly what you'll do. Isn't it? Take me in, get him to interrogate me?"

"No, it isn't. You have to trust me."

"Give me one good reason!"

Her blue eyes searched his. One good reason. He didn't have one, he realized. But he was . . . just sick and tired of being alone, and they could help each other, he was sure of it.

"Well, well, isn't this interesting?" A man's voice cut through the silence between them.

Van Meegeren was standing in the doorway, dressed in a thick woolen overcoat and a mink hat. He casually raised the black revolver in his gloved hand.

"Before you get any silly ideas about running away or some such."

"Who is this?" Willa asked Tygo, her eyes widening with fear.

"Don't you remember me, Wilhelmina?"

Willa shook her head.

"An old friend of your mother's from before the war. I remember Viktor Löwenstein giving her the Red Queen when you were born. He said it was the second most beautiful thing in the world. Such a charming man, so rich."

Willa stared at van Meegeren, then glared at Tygo. "You brought him here!" she spat.

Now it was Tygo's turn to shake his head vehemently.

"No, let's be fair, that's not exactly true." Van Meegeren advanced into the hallway. "I'm afraid your friend here is a very bad liar. When your name came up in conversation today I got the distinct impression that Frettchen here had had the pleasure of making your acquaintance."

"I'm sorry," Tygo said to Willa, remembering how he had reacted at van Meegeren's house.

"Shut up," Willa replied.

"So I thought it might worth seeing if my suspicions were correct. Nothing ventured, nothing gained, as they say. And I am very glad I did. You are going to get me out of a lot of hot water."

"No!" Tygo knew instantly what van Meegeren had in mind. He was going to turn Willa in to Krüger.

"I'm sorry, it's nothing personal," van Meegeren went on. "It's just that Krüger is a dangerous man, and I like to keep on the right side of dangerous men. If you please, I have a car outside."

Neither Tygo nor Willa moved. Van Meegeren sighed, snapped the hammer of the revolver back, and fired. Tygo's police cap was blown off his head. He staggered back, shocked.

"The next one is two inches lower, Wilhelmina. Do you really want to see your knight in shining armor with a hole in his head?"

Willa looked over at Tygo, a mixture of anger and fear in her eyes. Any trust or friendship he might have built had turned to dust.

"I don't know anything," she said.

"Then you have nothing to fear." Van Meegeren smiled unpleasantly, just as he had when Tygo and Krüger had visited him. "Shall we?"

Willa walked slowly toward the front door. Tygo followed her, his head hanging. At the doorway Willa took one quick last look back inside the house. Tygo could see she knew she was never coming back.

Van Meegeren owned a Hansa 1100. It was a small navy-blue sedan, still looking like it had just left the showroom. He had to be one of the few private citizens not working for the authorities who could still run a car. Selling art and information to the Nazis was clearly a profitable business to be in. It also stank. Tygo didn't like to think what would happen to van Meegeren once the war was over.

"Get in," ordered van Meegeren, twisting the chrome handle.

It was pitch-black inside the trunk of the car. Tygo and Willa were crammed tightly together, like two spoons, with Tygo's back against the rear seat.

The car started up after a couple of coughs and pulled away, van Meegeren changing the gears heavily.

"What are we going to do?" Willa hissed. She didn't sound scared, just angry, thought Tygo. Perhaps that was a good thing.

"I don't know, I'm thinking. We haven't got much time; it's not far to Headquarters." Tygo felt inside his tunic pocket and found a loose match. "Hang on."

He struck the match on the inside of the trunk lid, and it flared brightly. The car slid around a corner and Tygo was forced even closer to Willa. She jabbed him in the ribs. The match burned Tygo's fingers.

"Ow!" He lit another and noticed a bit of old sacking wrapped around something by the wheel arch. He leaned over Willa and pulled it toward him. He saw it was a small metal jack, the kind used to lift the car up if there was a puncture. Then the match went out.

"Quick, shift places with me."

"Why?"

"Just do it if you want me to get us out of here!" Tygo said, losing patience.

Willa rolled onto her back and Tygo slid across her as best he could. He found the jack with his hands in the dark, and wedged it between the floor of the trunk and the lid. He quickly started to turn the metal handle and felt the jack starting to scissor up until the top part made contact with the lid.

The car had pulled to a halt. "Are we here?" asked Willa.

"We can't be yet . . ."

Sure enough, the car set off again, turning another corner. Tygo was now twisting the handle slowly, the pressure building on the lid. Suddenly there was a sharp snap and the catch on the lock gave way. The lid flipped up a couple of inches and Tygo could see out. They were driving through Merwedeplein, getting close to Gestapo HQ.

The car slowed as it reached the bridge over the south Amstel canal. Tygo glanced back at Willa. "Let's go!" Without giving her the chance to argue, he grabbed her arm and yanked her forward, pushing the lid up. They both fell in a heap on the ground, rolling along the icy tarmac.

Tygo was already pulling Willa down the road before the car came to a halt and an astonished van Meegeren got out. He shouted vainly after them, but didn't give chase. It wouldn't have done any good; he would never have caught them.

Ten minutes later Tygo hurried down the stone steps leading to the frozen canal. He was carrying his skates, along with the pistol he had taken from Ursula. Thinking on his feet, he had come up with a plan, and the pistol meant that nobody was going to stop him.

Willa was still there waiting for him, tucked back between two storage huts on the towpath.

He smiled at her with relief. "I wasn't sure you'd still be here."

"I wasn't sure myself," she replied.

"I'm going to make it up to you, I swear." He sat down and quickly took off his boots, strapping on the skates. It was after three o'clock and the light was fading fast.

"Trust me, this is the safest way for us to get to my shop." He stepped down onto the frozen ice.

"What am I supposed to do, fly?" asked Willa.

"No, stupid, climb on my back. I'm strong."

Willa looked at him for a moment, then stepped forward and landed on his back with a little jump. Tygo struggled to keep upright for a second or two, then found his balance.

The terrible winter had taken its toll on Willa, and she was so thin and light that Tygo could easily carry her. He pushed off firmly, and within a few confident strides they were skimming along the frozen surface. He hugged the sides of the moored-up barges and canal boats. The light of oil lamps shone through some portholes as darkness continued to fall.

Willa tightened her grip around his neck with her arms, her legs around his waist as he built up the pace. Tygo swung his arms to keep up the momentum.

"This is great!" Willa laughed into his ear, and he tried to put on some extra speed. He wondered for a moment if he would make it, but he was determined not to fail Willa again. By the time they reached the Armbrug bridge, Tygo's legs felt like jelly.

"I didn't think you could do that," said Willa as he set her down.

"Piece of cake," said Tygo, fighting for breath. "Now, listen." He started to unlace his skates. "Once you're safely in the shop, I have to get back to Headquarters right away before Krüger misses me."

"I understand." Tygo could see she had almost forgiven him from before.

Tygo pulled on his boots. "There are some metal rungs in the wall." He pointed, and followed Willa as she started to climb up by the side of the bridge.

Once they had reached the street, they went around to the back of the shop and shimmied over the high wall using the rope that Tygo had left behind when he escaped on Christmas Day. Nothing had changed at Winter's Locksmiths since, including his bedroom door that the Resistance had smashed down.

"You'll be safe here," he said. "The Resistance know I don't live here now. There's no food, I'm afraid, but I'll bring what I can when I come back."

"You're coming back?" Willa was staring at him skeptically.

"Yes, of course," Tygo said.

"Look, I told that man and I'm telling you, I don't know anything about this diamond, this Red Queen!"

"Really?" Tygo tried to hide the note of disappointment in his voice.

"Really. So there's no point, is there, in coming back?"

"You know, you're a very hard person to be friends with."

"We're not friends."

Tygo stood there a moment longer; he could be as stubborn as she was, he decided.

"Well, I'm coming back," he said, "like it or lump it."

"Suit yourself," she said.

"Fine."

"Good."

If the door had still been on its hinges, Tygo would have slammed it on his way out.

11

Tygo made it back to Headquarters by five. The elevator wasn't working again, so he sprinted up the stone stairs to the third floor. His legs just about made it. Since the events of the afternoon he had been running on adrenaline.

Krüger was still inside his office. The door was open, as was often the way to let the cigarette smoke out, rather than opening a window to the frigid air. Tygo stood in the doorway, and Krüger glanced at him after a couple of moments and waved him in.

"Where have you been?"

"Back to my parents' shop, to fetch some extra tools."

Krüger nodded, and Tygo started to get a bad feeling inside. Had van Meegeren already been to see him? he wondered. But no—it seemed unlikely he would come here to tell Krüger he had failed.

Krüger got up from his desk and crossed to the large safe. He unlocked it and took out a velvet pouch before quickly locking the safe again. "We've been busy, you and I, these last six months. Here, take a look."

Krüger returned to his desk and tipped the pouch. A cascade of flashing, iridescent diamonds waterfalled out onto his ink blotter.

"Do you know what these are?"

Tygo nodded—of course he knew.

"My future." Krüger cupped a cluster in his palm. "Fate—or rather General Müller—has given me the chance today to secure a very pleasant one." He fished a small metal tin from his drawer and carefully measured half of the diamonds into it. The rest he returned in their pouch to the safe.

Again Tygo watched Krüger turn the key in the lock and place the key back in his pocket. He unconsciously put his own hands in his pockets, and felt the plug of potter's clay from the day before.

"Where were you going last night?" Krüger asked the question lightly.

"I don't know what you mean."

"You surrendered to a sector twelve patrol in the small hours. What were you doing?"

Tygo felt his face becoming hot.

"Lie to me and I will have you shot."

"I was going back to the villa."

Krüger stared at him, and Tygo could see his mind working. "Van Meegeren spoke of a girl."

Tygo had to decide what to say. Clearly Krüger already had his suspicions; he had checked up on his movements the night before, and had listened to van Meegeren.

"She was in the house, up the chimney."

Krüger walked around from behind his desk. He struck Tygo hard across the face, the first time he had ever done such a thing. Tygo fell back onto the floor, felt his mouth fill with a warm metallic taste.

"Where is she? Does she have the stone?"

Tygo shook his head, his cheek burning. "She wasn't there. I don't know where she is. She must have run, I swear."

Tygo hoped Krüger would believe him. He swallowed the blood and started to get back up, but Krüger grabbed ahold of his collar and hauled him to his feet. God, the man was strong. Tygo had never realized.

"Are you lying?"

"She wasn't there! Why would I lie to you? I went to find the stone for you!" Tygo shouted. "For you!"

Krüger's eyes bored into Tygo's, then his grip around his neck began to relax. The Oberst let him go and took a step back, thinking.

"She must have it. That's why she ran. When we return, you and I are going to find her."

Tygo nodded, then frowned. "Return? We're going somewhere, Herr Oberst?"

Krüger nodded. "You don't imagine for one moment I am going to let you out of my sight now?" He pocketed the small tin of diamonds and picked up the black attaché case that General Müller had brought with him.

Outside it was bitterly cold. Krüger's Opel was accompanied by an armored car in front and behind. He was taking no chances. Krüger dropped the case into a metal box, closed the lid, and secured the metal latches. "Bulletproof and fireproof," he said before slamming the trunk lid. They clambered inside and the convoy moved off. For a moment, Tygo could have sworn he saw Ursula across the street, huddled in a doorway, but when he looked again no one was there.

They sat in silence as the vehicles made their way through the city, sirens wailing plaintively. It was a horrible sound. Another freezing night would embrace the city, and the terrible winter would gun down a fresh squad of victims.

"Where are we going?" Tygo asked, his cheek still stinging.

"Wait and see," replied Krüger, lighting a cigarette.

Twenty minutes later, a partial answer was provided to Tygo's question as the convoy was waved through the security barrier at Schiphol, the city's main airfield. It was heavily fortified with wire fences and watchtowers, and Tygo could see bomb craters pockmarking the whole area. The convoy's lights cut a narrow path past a line of German fighters and assorted Junker transports, all covered with snow, before driving into a hangar behind the control tower.

"Bring the box," Krüger said, climbing out.

Tygo did as he was told and followed Krüger toward the aircraft parked inside the hangar. It was a huge four-engine bomber, the wing positioned on top of the fuselage and with a twin tail. It was the biggest plane Tygo had ever seen, its undercarriage wheels as big as tractor tires. It was painted a matte black and had simple white stars on its wings and tail.

"An American B-24 Liberator bomber, before you ask," said Krüger. "A lot safer for flying over enemy territory."

The normal crew of eleven had been reduced to nine to accommodate the two passengers. The pilot walked across in light-blue Luftwaffe flying overalls. He was wearing a bright orange life jacket around his neck like a stuffed fox.

"American?" said Tygo, staring at the plane.

"*Ja*, captured in Italy, ran out of fuel," replied the pilot, before saluting Krüger smartly. "Werner Baumbach, commander of Kampfgeschwader 200, at your disposal, Herr Oberst."

Krüger returned the salute smartly. "A great honor," he said. Tygo thought he sounded almost deferential.

"And where do we have the pleasure of taking you tonight?" Baumbach asked.

Krüger reached into his jacket and took out a buff envelope, which he handed to Baumbach. "Your flight plan and instructions are here. How soon can we fly?"

"We are almost ready for you now—perhaps a little more fuel, depending on the destination. Please climb aboard; we have fitted two seats in the waist gunner's compartments. I will have some coffee and sandwiches loaded for you."

"Thank you, Oberstleutnant. What about the package?"

"There is a special compartment for it inside the plane. Do you wish one of my men to load it?"

"No, we'll take it on board."

"We're going too?" said Tygo, surprised.

"Didn't I mention that?" said Krüger with a thin smile.

Tygo and Krüger had been allocated the midsection of the bomber for their seats and the safe carriage of Krüger's cargo. There was a floor-mounted metal compartment into which the metal box fit. It was armored, one of the crew members said as he helped Tygo slot it in. After that, the crew member showed Krüger and Tygo their seats, which had been bolted just behind the large Perspex windows that served as firing positions for the plane's midsection pair of heavy-caliber waist guns. There were American AN/M2 .50 caliber machine guns with a gun heater near the breach and a K-13 compensating sight at the back near the trigger button.

The Perspex windows were latched closed, but the crew

member demonstrated to them how, if the plane were to come under attack, they were to fix the windows open and slide the gun around into the opening. He showed them how to work the gun, the cocking handle and firing button, before sliding the gun back and relatching the window closed. Next, he helped them both to pull on their flying coveralls, thick sheepskin coats, and leather flying caps and goggles, and showed them how to put on the oxygen masks and work the radio. Finally he helped them pull on their parachutes and snap the stiff four-point harnesses into the heavy steel buckles.

Tygo felt like some gigantic beetle in danger of toppling over and not being able to right itself. Krüger didn't look too comfortable either.

"Don't worry about the parachute," the crew member laughed as he climbed back down through the plane's belly hatch, "you'll be dead long before you ever get to use it!"

The hatch was slammed closed by their feet, and Krüger and Tygo sat in their seats on either side of the fuselage. Tygo found he was sweating. He managed to lean forward and stare out the window, the oxygen mask swinging loose from one side of his flying cap. Listening to the ground crew shouting final orders, and then the high-pitched whine of the starter motors, followed by the heavy cough of the big engines as they caught, and finally the blast of noise as each one burst into life, Tygo forgot all his fears and was caught up in the excitement of the moment. He had never in his whole life been on a plane.

He pressed his face against the window as the craft suddenly lurched forward and then started to roll over the concrete, thumping on the ridges in it, gathering speed. After a couple of minutes, the tail of the plane suddenly swung around and the engines roared much louder. The plane accelerated hard, and Tygo could see a few lights flashing past . . . then, with a last thud, it was free of the ground and climbing up steeply into the darkness.

Tygo was pressed back into his seat. He gripped the arms and stared ahead as the plane plowed forward at an alarmingly steep degree; it almost felt like they were falling rather than climbing. He fumbled for the lap belt fitted to the seat and managed to clip the two parts together.

He tried to adjust to this new sensation of flying. It was like nothing he'd ever experienced: He felt tethered but at the same time strangely weightless. There was no clackety-clack of train wheels over points, just the throb of the engines and the faint whistling sound of rushing air.

But then the plane started to bounce, like a speedboat hitting a swell. The engine roared louder. Tygo cried out in alarm.

"It's just turbulence, Frettchen," Krüger yelled across to him. "It's nothing."

But it didn't feel like nothing as the giant bomber suddenly shot up through the air. Then it was over; Tygo could see that they were above the clouds now. He felt his heart hammering inside his chest. He glanced over at Krüger, who was smoking a cigarette, taking in deep lungfuls of smoke. Of course, he'd probably been on planes lots of times, Tygo thought.

After about ten minutes, the plane performed a long, slow bank, rolling onto its left side. Leaning forward, Tygo thought he could see the sea shifting below them, the tops of the waves iridescent. He wondered what it must be like to crash into it at hundreds of miles an hour.

He turned and checked on Krüger again. He had wedged a blanket between the fuselage and his seat and was resting his head on it, his eyes closed. His nonchalance made Tygo relax. Everything would be all right, he told himself.

He stared ahead down the fuselage, past the gun positions. There was a solid bulkhead with a small hatch to allow a crew member to crawl through to the next section of the plane. It started to get very cold, and Tygo clipped on the oxygen mask and pulled on a pair of heavy fleece-lined mittens, then yanked the goggles down over his eyes. He felt a lot better now. He didn't have a pillow, but he propped his head against the side of the plane and closed his eyes. It had been a very, very long day.

He slept fitfully, waking every half hour with a sudden start, gasping at the oxygen in the mask, feeling like he was being pushed underwater. When he opened his eyes again, it felt like the plane was descending. Tygo looked out the window, but could see absolutely nothing, just a thick white fog. They must be in cloud, he realized, but there was a gentle pressure on his back, pushing him forward against his lap belt, and the floor of the plane was tilting down.

"Soon be there!" Krüger yelled to him from the other side of the fuselage. He had a steaming mug of coffee in his hand and another cigarette in the other. He put the cigarette in his mouth, leaned down, and rolled the thermos flask across the plane. Tygo unscrewed the cap and tried to sip the hot liquid inside. It wasn't coffee after all, but it was very sweet and hot and it perked him up a bit.

He looked out the window again. They seemed to be descending faster, and Tygo heard a whizzing of hydraulics and grinding of gears as the undercarriage was deployed. Below him he could see the sea again, and the lights of a city, bright lights twinkling in their thousands. It was incredible— where on earth could they have reached that had no blackout? He could see streets and individual buildings all lit up, and ships, hundreds of them all along the docks. It was amazing.

The name on the main airport building read AEROPUERTO DE BARCELONA. Spain. They had flown to Spain! That would explain the lights: Spain was a neutral country in the war.

They taxied past the airport building and continued until they reached a part of the apron far from the rest of the planes and buildings. Tygo unstrapped his belt and stood up, a little wobbly, but feeling excited at this turn of events. The plane came to a final halt and the engines were switched off, the propellers starting to wind down. Krüger unlatched the hatch door and dropped down through it.

"Hand me the package," he shouted up to Tygo.

Tygo did as he was told, unlashing the metal box and carefully handing it down through the hatch. He waited there, and Krüger looked up at him.

"Well? What are you waiting for?"

Tygo dropped through the hatch onto the tarmac. It was a little after midnight, but the night air was completely different from Amsterdam. There was still a smell of the fuel and rubber, but also the briny tang of the sea and something else, like a spice, almost. It was so much warmer too, perhaps fifty degrees.

Baumbach had climbed down from the cockpit and was walking across to them.

"Congratulations, Oberstleutnant," said Krüger, "you got us here in one piece." The two men saluted each other.

"And I will get you back in one piece too!" He grinned jauntily, his flying cap askew. Tygo noticed the Iron Cross with Oak Leaves around his neck. He looked very handsome and brave, he thought.

"Excellent," replied Krüger. "We need to leave in two hours—you will be ready?" He started to strip off all his flying gear and Tygo followed suit.

"Of course—we might even have time for a little paella and a jug or two of sangria, eh, boys?" The rest of his crew, who had gathered around, shouted their approval of that idea.

They all turned at the sound of vehicles approaching. The lead vehicle was a large Hispano-Suiza J12, a four-door luxury car. Behind it were an army jeep and truck. The vehicles stopped, and soldiers clambered out of the back.

Baumbach began to unhook the retaining button on his holster.

"Please, Commander, don't be alarmed," said Krüger. "They are here to protect us. It has all been arranged. It is not often an American bomber lands on neutral territory."

The soldiers fanned out around the plane, taking up picket duty. From the Hispano emerged a small, very distinguished-looking man dressed in the robes of a Catholic priest. He had a large silver cross on a chain around his neck and he was wearing a biretta, a stiff, square-shaped silk hat with trim and tuft. It was purple, the color for a bishop—Tygo knew that. He walked with a silver-topped cane.

"Welcome to Barcelona," he said in German. His skin was the color of caramel, his voice like butter. "The señorita is expecting you."

12

It was going to be a long night of firsts for Tygo. First time on a plane, and now first time inside such a ludicrously luxurious motorcar. The interior was lined with the softest calf leather, the doors fitted with rosewood panels, and dark-blue Wilton carpet lay on the floor. There was a bottle of champagne in an ice bucket and two crystal goblets. A polished silver voice trumpet connected the passengers in the rear seat to the driver up front.

The chauffeur started the engine and they pulled away. The car was whisper-quiet and super-fast. They whistled out of the airport and along the deserted streets of the city. The metal box sat between the two men on the rear seats, Tygo facing them on a fold-down seat behind the driver's partition.

The two men talked occasionally in mutters, with a lot of nodding on Krüger's part, and Tygo was content to stare out at the houses, so different from those of his hometown. How wonderful it was to be in a city at peace. *No death, no destruction, just like it used to be back home*, he thought.

He didn't even notice how long it was before the car pulled to a halt outside a grand-looking French-style building of ten or more stories. The bishop picked up the speech trumpet and spoke to the driver, and the car moved off again, turning the corner and making a series of further turns until it pulled into the alley behind the hotel.

"A little more discreet, don't you think?" the bishop said to Krüger. "We don't want any prying eyes to report your arrival, do we?"

"British?"

"British, American, French, Russian, they're all here. The place is crawling with spies."

The chauffeur opened the door and they climbed out.

Tygo had been in quite a few fancy hotel rooms in his time. His father was sometimes called out—before the war, of course—when a rich guest lost the key to their strongbox or couldn't remember the combination to their safe. But Tygo had never seen such a hotel room as the one they were ushered into now by the chauffeur. It wasn't a room at all, but a series of rooms: lounges filled with exquisite furnishings, huge crystal chandeliers, and thick, rich carpet. It was like being inside a royal palace.

The bishop had left them both standing in the first room and disappeared through one of the interconnecting doors.

89

Tygo was still looking around in amazement when another door on the opposite side opened and a woman in a dazzling gown appeared.

She looked around forty and held a cigarette in a long ebony holder. Her blond hair was tied back, and for some reason she was wearing dark glasses, even though it was the middle of the night. Tygo noticed the four strands of diamonds around her neck. Perhaps that was the reason for the dark glasses, to shield her from the dazzle when the stones hit the light. Tygo felt drawn to her presence; she exuded some sort of power, like a film star. Yes, that was what she was like.

Krüger clicked his heels and bowed formally. The woman offered him her hand, and he leaned down and kissed the top of it.

"A great honor," he said in Spanish. "General Müller sends his compliments; he would have wished to be here personally if he could, Señorita Perón."

"Duarte, I am Eva Duarte," she laughed back at him, a throaty laugh from cigarettes and singing. Wine too. "But I think soon my beloved general will make an honest woman of me, before he is president." She laughed again; it seemed to come easily to her. "And if all of this goes well, then that will be very soon."

She looked at Tygo now, and the steel box he was holding.

"Have you brought me something nice, young man?" Krüger was amused to see Tygo blush. She used her index finger to draw him closer. "Come into my boudoir and we shall see."

They followed her from the first reception room to a second one, which seemed even larger, talking in Spanish as they went. Tygo might understand something of what was going on—but Krüger didn't want him knowing everything.

"Open the case," he said to the boy in German, then handed the señorita a letter. She indicated that they should sit together on a large velvet sofa.

Tygo unlatched the metal box and took out the attaché case, placing it on the glass-topped table in front of the woman. She put the letter down, then leaned forward and unlatched the case. Reaching in, she pulled out the thick bundle of paper from within, fanning the sheets in her hands.

"United States treasury bearer bonds, each one for ten thousand dollars," said Krüger.

"Are they real?" The same laugh.

Krüger was offended, but covered it with a laugh of his own. "Not only real, but good in any country in the world. Better than cash itself."

The señorita put down the bundle and picked up the letter again. "Excellent—then I will write a receipt!" She stood and crossed to a writing table. "Please assure General Müller that all arrangements have been made for the Führer and his party as agreed. After I have visited His Holiness, I will be returning to Buenos Aires by the sixteenth and I will be there with General Perón, ready and waiting."

She finished writing a short note and folded it into an envelope.

"There remains only one matter outstanding."

"The Red Queen?" Krüger preempted.

The woman slipped the dark glasses down her nose for the first time, exposing hard, black eyes.

"When General Müller first approached us many months ago," she said, "he asked me in private what the Führer could give me as a token for all our help and support. 'Give me the Red Queen,' I said, and the good general just nodded and smiled, and then he said, 'The day the Führer greets you in Argentina he will place the Red Queen around your neck. I give you my word.'"

Krüger couldn't resist using this moment as an opportunity to ingratiate himself with the woman; after all, her future husband would be running Argentina in a couple of months. "I hope you will not think I am being boastful, but I am the officer whom the general entrusted to find the stone."

"You?" Eva Duarte looked at Krüger with something approaching real interest now.

"Yes, in Amsterdam."

"And you have it?"

"Yes," he lied.

She clapped her hands together in excitement. "Is it as beautiful as they say?"

"More—it is like yourself, flawless."

"You are a charming young man, Oberst."

Krüger smiled his most charming smile. "Please, I have my own little token for you."

He took out the small metal tin and handed it to the woman. She opened the lid and stared at the diamonds inside. After a moment or two she looked back at Krüger with fresh appreciation.

"Charming *and* generous, it would seem. I wonder perhaps if there is anything you would like in return."

"Just the opportunity to serve you and the general in any way I can."

"Is that so? Well, I'm sure we can arrange that. Will you be traveling with the others?"

Krüger nodded; come hell or high water, he was getting on that plane.

"Excellent—then let us toast before you go." Eva walked across and poured some spirit into two small glasses. "To the future," she said.

"*Zukunft*," Krüger replied, repeating the word in German. They downed their drinks in one and he kissed her hand again.

A most successful evening for all concerned, he thought.

13

The crew of the bomber was already back on board and the engines were idling by the time the limousine raced across the airfield and slewed to a halt. It was still dark, around four o'clock in the morning, with a crisp breeze blowing off the sea. Krüger and Tygo climbed back up into the belly of the plane and closed off the hatch.

Krüger picked up the microphone to the internal intercom. "We're ready to depart, Oberstleutnant Baumbach."

The Liberator's four engines gradually rose in pitch and the big bomber rolled forward, taxiing for takeoff. Tygo and Krüger struggled back into their flying uniforms and the heavy jackets, helmets, goggles, parachutes, and the rest. By the time they had sat down in their seats the plane was racing down the runway, and then it was into the air.

Tygo craned his neck to see the city falling away to the left as the bomber swung north toward the French coast. He thought about the strange meeting he'd witnessed, and wished he spoke Spanish. He'd been surprised by Krüger's fluency in the language. But he understood something very clearly: They were toasting the future—he knew the German word—and it was obvious that Krüger had somehow secured a very bright one for himself as a result of this meeting.

He settled back in his seat and snapped on his oxygen like an old pro. He was so tired that almost immediately the rocking of the plane and the drone of the engines were pulling him under like the finest mesmerist. He knew he ought to be thinking, working out what to do when he got back.

What to do. What to do.

A searing pain ripped Tygo awake. It felt like someone had placed a red-hot poker over his forearm. For a moment he didn't know where he was—it was pitch-black, there was a terrible banging noise, and he was being pushed and pulled in his seat by some unseen force. Almost immediately he realized what was happening: The plane was under attack and he had been shot.

He looked at his left arm, where the pain was. His thick leather flying jacket had been sliced through like a hot knife through butter. Beneath it was a neat crimson line across his forearm where the muscle had been sliced open, not quite down to the bone. Blood was pouring out. Beside him, a hole had been punched through the metal fuselage, and as Tygo looked, he saw a fresh series of them blossom down the side like exclamation points.

"Night fighters! Frettchen, man that gun!" Krüger was yelling at him, and Tygo came fully awake.

The plane was rolling and pitching, and there was the sound of multiple machine guns being fired from the other gun positions in the plane. It was like being on a ship under attack in a wild storm. *Repel all boarders!*

Tygo undid his belt and pulled himself up. He staggered forward and managed to get the Perspex window latched open. Then he swung the heavy machine gun around and shoved the barrel out into the night air. A belt of ammunition was already fed into the gun's breech and the cocking lever pulled back. The noise from the engines and the guns was simply deafening, and Tygo hung on to the machine gun's handles for dear life as the slipstream threatened to suck him clean out of the plane. He glanced over at Krüger, whose gun was chattering out into the darkness, blobs of tracer arcing out.

"I've been shot!" Tygo yelled, but his reply went unheard. Krüger continued firing wildly out into the night.

The plane suddenly banked steeply and Tygo almost fell to one side, just managing to brace himself against the machine gun to stay on his feet. He stared out the window, and suddenly a great black shape shot past, less than fifty yards away. He pressed the trigger and bullets spewed out, white tracers pulsing their way toward the shape. It was gone. He stopped firing. He stared out into the sky again, desperate to find the attacking plane. Their own plane was slewing across the sky now, Baumbach obviously trying to make it less of a sitting duck.

Tygo looked out into the darkness toward the tail fins of the bomber. There! Just below him, a shape was coming up very fast. Suddenly white sparkles lit up in a row: Its nose cannons were firing. Tygo swung the compensator gun sight around and lined up on those white flames.

He pressed the trigger and the gun erupted. Empty brass and chain link waterfalled down, making a hot smoking pile of metal around his feet. The plane kept coming straight toward him, and he was certain its propeller would slice him to ribbons. But he kept firing; it felt like his finger was welded to the fire control button. Then there was a massive orange fireball where the plane had been, and it was gone. The force blew Tygo back into the plane. He grabbed his chair.

"I got it!" he yelled. His heart was thumping so fast.

"Stay there!" barked Krüger. "There may be others."

Tygo nodded, glancing at his arm. The bleeding seemed to have stopped during the action, and so had the pain. But now it returned, a burning fire. He stood clinging on to the gun, staring out at the sky, and tried to ignore it. He stood there, watching the sky as the darkness turned to dawn. Stood there until he was chilled to the bone and his eyes were aching and his face blue with cold.

Only when the plane started to sink down and the coastline came into view below the clouds did Krüger order him to stand down and return to his seat.

As the bomber thumped down onto the runway Tygo felt a wave of relief, promptly followed by a wave of nausea. As soon as he was out of the hatch, he fell to his knees and was violently sick on the ground. He wiped his mouth and slowly got back up. The rest of the crew were climbing out. The plane itself was riddled with bullet holes. Tygo noticed the tail gunner's turret was shot to pieces and the gunner was no longer lying inside.

Krüger walked across to him. "Come on, Frettchen, pull yourself together." He took hold of Tygo's arm and examined the wound. "It's not so bad—missed the vein. We'll get it dressed at Headquarters."

Tygo nodded. He saw that Krüger's car was already there waiting to take them into the city and stumbled toward it while Krüger spoke to Baumbach.

"Oberstleutnant, I will tell General Müller you have performed exceptional service for the Führer today."

The two men saluted each other, then Tygo and Krüger climbed into Krüger's waiting Opel Admiral. Tygo cradled his injured arm; it felt like it was on fire. Krüger glanced at him as the car set off across the runway apron.

"Get that wound attended to and some food inside you as soon as we get back," he said. "It is now almost eight in the morning, and you have till midnight to find me that girl. She is the key to finding that stone, of that I am sure."

Tygo nodded. "Yes, Oberst Krüger. I will do my best."

"There is no best here, Frettchen, there is only success and failure. Understand?"

With that, Krüger tilted his cap down over his eyes and leaned his head against the window of the car.

Tygo sat there, the pain and the fear preventing him from sleeping. After a few minutes, Krüger began to snore softly. Tygo looked over at him, then, with a surge of excitement and fear, noticed Krüger's leather key case sticking halfway out of his trouser pocket.

He put his hand in his own pocket. The lump of potter's clay was still there.

Slowly he slid closer across the backseat. He started to knead the clay and, as he was doing so, reached very slowly out with his other hand and slid the key case out of Krüger's pocket. In seconds he had the safe key out and pressed deep into the lump of clay, taking an impression. Carefully he removed the key from the clay, and eased it and the case back into the Oberst's pocket.

Krüger suddenly shifted in his seat and Tygo shot back to his side of the car. The clay was safely back in his pocket. He didn't know when he might get the chance to investigate the contents of Krüger's safe, but it was at least a chance.

14

Tygo, his arm freshly dressed and his stomach full of hot porridge, made it back to his father's shop by ten o'clock. For a change the sun was actually shining and the skies were a tepid January blue. He entered through the back door.

"Willa, it's me, Tygo," he called out softly.

But there was only silence.

Tygo hurried upstairs and searched the bedrooms, but there was no sign of her. He came back down and walked across to the hearth. Someone had lit a small fire in the grate in front of the shop's counter, the ash still warm. He looked around.

Then he saw it on the counter: a piece of folded paper with a blank key resting on top of it, keeping it secure. He unfolded it and read the short message.

"Ursula." Tygo spat the name out. Of course it was she, together with those boys, who had taken Willa. They must have still been watching the shop after all, just in case he ever returned. Well, Tygo thought, they wouldn't win. He'd get her back. But first he had one task to complete.

He retrieved the clay from his pocket and hurried into the rear workshop at the back of the shop. It was very small, and the workbench was still covered with all the different paraphernalia needed for locksmithing. Tygo selected a small crucible and placed a small quantity of Wood's metal into it. There was no gas for the Bunsen burner, but this particular alloy—a mixture of bismuth, lead, tin, and cadmium—melted at 158 degrees Fahrenheit, so the little paraffin stove would do the job.

Tygo got it going and watched as the alloy slowly dissolved into a small pool of quivering silver, then he picked it up with some tongs and, very slowly and carefully, poured it into the impression he had made in the clay. Wood's metal was also very quick to cool, and after a few minutes Tygo was able to cut through the lump of clay and split it into two. There, inside one half, was a perfect metal copy of Krüger's safe key. Tygo stashed it safely in his trouser pocket. He could feel it, still warm, against his leg.

Now all he needed was to find Willa. And the diamond. Ideally in that order.

He left the shop through the front door, leaving it unlocked. There was no point in trying to stay hidden, after all; the sooner Ursula showed her face the better. He cut across to Damrak and walked away from the station until he reached Dam Square and the Royal Palace. He decided to hang around there for a little while. Before the war the square had been filled with people every day, enjoying the myriad cafés and restaurants, feeding the pigeons. Now it was almost deserted, and certainly the pigeons were not taking any chances: They would make a delicious meal.

After about ten minutes, he noticed a group of three young boys staring at him. They were dressed in filthy cast-offs, and two of them had makeshift drums hanging from their necks, made from empty cookie tins with holes punched in the sides for the twine used as a strap. Instead of drumsticks they had pieces of kindling. The lead boy had a tin whistle. Whenever Tygo looked at them, they glanced away or pretended to gaze into the empty shop windows. Typical lookouts, he thought— the drums and whistle were to signal danger.

He strode across to them. "You boys!" he barked, in his best imitation of Krüger. He reached into his pocket and took out the Gestapo warrant disk. "I want to speak to you."

The boys turned and fled.

"If she wants me, I'm here!" Tygo yelled after them. He turned and went to stand out of the wind by the Gothic New Church. The bell tolled eleven. Time was ticking.

He didn't have to wait long. Presently Ursula cycled into the square and made a couple of circuits, looking for Tygo. After her second pass he stepped out and made himself visible to her. A line for the soup kitchen was beginning to form on the other side of the church.

Ursula dismounted as she got closer and walked the last few feet to Tygo. She had the most self-satisfied smile on her face, and Tygo felt a terrible red mist descending. He took a couple of steps toward her.

"You lay a finger on me, I swear you'll never see that girl again," she said.

Tygo stopped and took a deep breath. The bandage over Ursula's nose looked fresh. Where would she get such a thing in this city? Tygo suddenly wondered.

"You've handed her to the Resistance, haven't you?"

"Who's a clever boy, then?"

Tygo stared at Ursula. He felt so angry but at the same time he understood what she had done. Perhaps if circumstances were different he would have acted the same.

"And when you go to get her, I'll get my money." She laughed unpleasantly.

Tygo fought to keep his anger under control. "You know where she is?"

The girl nodded.

"Take me there."

Ursula frowned at Tygo for a long moment. "You want to

tell me what's so special about your girlfriend that you'd risk your life for her?"

"No," said Tygo. "And she's not my girlfriend."

It took a while before they reached their destination. Ursula was taking no chances and doubled back on their route a couple of times. Eventually Tygo found himself in the old Jewish quarter of the town, now largely deserted and abandoned. A few solitary figures shuffled along the sidewalks, pushing the little wooden foraging carts. The two of them had made the entire journey in silence, and that suited Tygo fine.

Tygo spotted the same three boys from Dam Square, and when they suddenly started to play their instruments he knew they must be close to where Willa was being held.

It turned out that the Resistance safe house was in fact an old factory building with heavy industrial sliding doors to the front. Cut into one of them was a small door with a black grille and inspection hatch.

Ursula knocked three times on the door and waited. After a moment the hatch slid back and a face appeared.

"Bob," said the man.

"Hope," said Ursula.

The bolts were drawn back and the door opened. Tygo and Ursula lifted their bikes through. A young man with a straggly beard was standing just inside, a British Sten gun slung over one shoulder and a bandolier of grenades over the other. He looked at Tygo like he wanted to punch him.

"Scum," he hissed. Tygo felt his cheeks color. "Follow me."

It was dark inside the building, but Tygo could make out an abandoned workshop beyond and rows of what looked like printing presses. No paper, no work. The young man shoved him in the ribs with the muzzle of the Sten, and Tygo kept walking, Ursula bringing up the rear.

"You wait here!" the guard said to Ursula.

"What about my money?" she said.

"I don't know anything about that," the guard replied. He indicated for Tygo to climb the steel staircase to the landing above the printing presses where the offices were. They stopped outside one of the offices. The words ACCOUNTS DEPT were painted on the door.

"Inside."

Tygo stepped in, the door slamming behind him. Willa looked up from the cot she had been lying on and sprang to her feet.

"Tygo!" she exclaimed. "You're alive."

"Alive and kicking," Tygo said. She was pleased to see him, it seemed, and he realized he was pleased to see her again too. "Are you all right?"

"I'm fine, they've treated me well—food, drink—I just don't understand what's going on. Where have you been all this time?"

Tygo realized it had been nearly a whole day since they had seen each other.

"Barcelona. I've been to Barcelona."

"What?" Willa stared at him, unbelieving. "You mean in Spain?"

"I know it's incredible, but I promise you it's really true. There's something really big and secret going on at the moment. We went in this special plane to a hotel in Barcelona, where Krüger gave some sort of . . . money, I think it was, to a woman, a very important woman called Eva Duarte. She must have been from Argentina—I heard her say Buenos Aires."

"I've heard of her." Willa was frowning.

"On the way back we got attacked and I shot down a plane."

"I don't believe *that*." Willa punched him playfully on the arm.

"Ow!" Tygo yelped. "See? I even got shot!" He slipped off his coat and showed Willa his bandaged arm.

"Really? Does it hurt?"

"Yes, it does."

Willa looked at him. "What's happening, Tygo?"

Tygo sat down on the bed. What *was* happening? He tried to make sense of everything.

"It's complicated, Willa," he said at last, "but I'm pretty sure there's some big plan happening with Krüger, something to do with"—he lowered his voice—"Adolf Hitler and a general called Müller. He's head of the Gestapo. I heard him say the words 'Operation Black Sun' and tomorrow's date. Krüger needs to find the Red Queen by then, or he's in big trouble. He's sent me to find you—he's convinced you know where it might be."

Willa shook her head. "For the last time, I don't know."

"Are you sure? Anything . . . some little thing your mother may have mentioned, a place she used to go? If I can get him the stone I know he will set me free, and we can get away from the city together; we'll find a way, and two's better than one. Do you trust me?"

But before she could answer, the door swung open and a heavily built man in his twenties with a scruffy beard marched in. He was smoking the stub of a thick cigar and had a Colt .45 tucked in his belt. He was wearing a red velvet shirt with a white silk scarf tied around his neck. Tygo thought he looked like the Laughing Cavalier from the famous portrait by Frans Hals.

"Ah, how touching—the Nazi ferret comes to save his girlfriend."

Tygo got up. "For the last time, she's not my girlfriend!"

The man drove his fist into Tygo's stomach, and he pitched backward. "That's enough from a stinking stooge. I do the talking here."

Tygo tottered to his feet, winded. "Who are you?" he said, rubbing his stomach.

"Who am *I*?" boomed the man. "Who are *you*?"

"You know who I am."

"Do I? Are you some Nazi-loving collaborator who seeks to save his own skin by helping the Gestapo rob and plunder? Is that who you are?"

"You know I have no choice! It's that or get shot!"

"We all have a choice, Tygo Winter."

"Let us go," said Tygo.

"Let you go?" laughed the man. "Why on earth should I do that? And don't worry, I wouldn't waste a bullet on you, either. Come with me, both of you."

There was no choice. No time to wonder what was happening. Numbly, Tygo and Willa followed the man out of the room and along the metal walkway to the office at the end. This one was marked SALES. The man stopped outside the door.

"But first," he said, "there's someone who wants to see you, someone who made the *right* choice, Tygo."

Tygo tried to imagine who that might be. The man pushed open the door and shoved Tygo into the room.

Sitting behind a desk was a young woman. Her hair was cut very short like a boy's, and there was a livid red scar on one side of her face. But there was no doubting who it was.

It was Alisa, Tygo's sister.

15

The small electric train rattled along its narrow-gauge lines, taking its precious cargo from deep beneath the Austrian town of Sankt Georgen back up to the surface.

General Müller was sitting in the first open-topped wagon, his face pouring with sweat. The heat deep in these caverns was terrific, but he had insisted on seeing the incredible work-shops and laboratories that slave labor from the nearby Mauthausen concentration camps had built deep underground.

Entire factories were operating here; the new jet planes were built in special galleries. But most vital was the small, top-secret facility that had created the bomb now strapped to one of the wagons behind Müller. This bomb was just the first wonder weapon, the head scientist had assured him. They would produce many more. It seemed fitting to Müller that such a hellish thing had been made deep underground.

Ahead the tunnel was widening out into a large gallery, which linked up to other tunnels, all with their own narrow-gauge railways. Thousands of prisoners were being marched in and out through the entrance, their shifts beginning or ending. They were dressed in ragged striped pajamas and their faces were skull-like, nothing more than skin and bone. The facilities operated twenty-four hours a day.

So this was the policy of *"Vernichtung durch Arbeit"* in action.

Müller caught the acrid smell of the men as the train went past them and for a moment a wave of nausea seized him. He fought it back and only allowed himself to breathe freely once they were outside.

An army truck was waiting with escort jeeps and Müller watched as the wooden crate containing the bomb was carefully loaded onto the back of it. There was the usual paperwork to be signed in triplicate, and then Müller saluted the head scientist and climbed aboard the truck.

It was a short trip from the underground laboratory to the nearby airfield at Linz, and thankfully no daylight air raids to worry about. He had left Eva Braun and her sister Gretl there to have lunch. Gretl's husband, Hermann Fegelein, was the liaison officer between Hitler and Himmler.

The small convoy was waved through the police checkpoint at the airfield and drove directly into a hangar where a bomber was waiting. Once again, Müller supervised the loading of the wonder weapon into the plane. It would take off later that day and fly to Peenemünde, where it would pick up the rocket that would carry this precious payload. From there both bomb and rocket would be taken to the secret airfield outside Amsterdam, and then, finally, everything would be in place.

Müller checked his watch. There was just time for him to join the ladies for some strudel perhaps, and then they too must be on the road. He marched briskly across the snow-covered tarmac to the small cafeteria, smoke billowing from its cowled steel chimney.

The two women sat at a corner table, their lunch finished. A cozy fire blazed in the stove and pleasant folk music was playing on the radio.

Müller took off his hat. "Perhaps I might join you for a coffee?"

"That would be delightful," said Eva. "Did you conclude your business, Herr General?" Her eyes were bright and hard, her lips a line of deep vermilion.

Müller sat down. There was a small posy of flowers in a vase and a pretty linen tablecloth on the table. He remembered the hell on earth for hundreds of thousands of prisoners just a few miles away, then shrugged.

"Most satisfactorily," he said.

16

The thickset man, Tygo discovered, was called Pieter, and he was the leader of this particular Resistance cell. He left them alone. Just the three of them. It was an emotional reunion, and for the first time in as long as Tygo could remember, he had cried, broken down and really cried, great hacking sobs. He felt embarrassed that Willa was there, but he couldn't stop himself. It was like a great weight he hadn't realized was pressing down on him had been suddenly lifted.

After that, he felt calmer, and he and Willa sat together on a battered sofa. They listened as Alisa explained what had happened the day she was transported from the city.

"After they had gathered us all together, they marched us out of the city to the east. All the men and boys in one column and the women and girls in another. We must have walked thirty miles that day. It was scorching hot and there was no water. Anyone who protested was shot. Anyone who stopped walking was shot. Finally we arrived at the railhead. They herded us into two sheds and left us there for twenty-four hours. Then the train arrived with the wooden boxcars. They had to hose the insides down and pour gasoline inside—it was horrible, God knows where they'd come from. They issued each of us with fresh identity papers and informed us we were being sent to Germany as 'guest workers.' Well, that was when I knew I had to escape, or die trying."

Tygo and Willa listened, wide-eyed.

"Just as we were being loaded I saw my opportunity—there was a great crush around the loading ramp and I managed to roll underneath the wagon. Then I was able to wedge myself up over the wagon's axles, out of sight. They checked under the train before we left, but they didn't find me. It was night by the time we pulled out, and I managed to hang on for a few miles, then before the train could pick up speed, I let go and fell into the middle of the tracks. Unfortunately I hit something in the dark—might have been a nail head—and sliced my face." She pointed to the livid scar. "Anyway, I didn't hang around. I ran through the night and ended up hiding under a railway bridge. That was where the Resistance found me. They had come there to plant a bomb. That man, Pieter, he saved my life. He carried me all the way back to their safe house, got a doctor to stitch me up, found me penicillin when the wound went septic, nursed me back to health. When I was better, I knew two things: I couldn't go home, and I wanted to fight. I've been part of Pieter's unit ever since."

She stood up. "So that's why you're here. I wanted to get you away from that criminal Krüger and protect you before some other Resistance group really does shoot you down in the street. The war is nearly over, Tygo, and accounts are going to be settled. I got Pieter to agree to do it for me a few days ago— you've been a hard man to track down, haven't you? Ursula nearly got you a couple of times, but Willa here proved to be the bait we needed."

So Ursula was never going to kill him, Tygo realized. He didn't know how he felt about her now.

"Krüger has been keeping you busy, has he?"

Tygo nodded again, then he stood up too. "Thank you, Alisa." He stepped toward her and they hugged. "What you've done is amazing. You always protected me, didn't you?"

"You're my little brother." She pinched his cheek. "You're safe now—well, safer anyway."

Tygo looked at her and shook his head. "If only that were true, Alisa, but Krüger has ordered me to do one last thing for him. If I don't, he'll hunt me down."

"Oh, Tygo . . ."

"It's not my fault, and I need Willa with me—but I can't say why. I just need you to let us go. Please help me one more time."

Alisa sighed. "All right, let me talk to Pieter."

———

They found him down among the printing presses, cleaning a stripped-down Bren gun.

"Why on earth would I let some Nazi collaborator slink back to his master only to tell him where he can find a group of Resistance fighters?" he said.

"I wouldn't do that!" Tygo said indignantly.

"And I'm supposed to take your word for it?"

"Don't take my word, take my sister's. She'll vouch for me."

"Your sister is a very brave young woman and the only reason that you are still standing in front of me and not strung up from a lamppost!" Pieter withdrew the cleaning rod from the barrel and held it up to the light to check it was clean. Satisfied, he started to reassemble the light machine gun.

Tygo's mind raced; there had to be something he could offer this brute.

"Information—what if I could get you some information?"

"Like what?"

"There's . . . there's a big operation being planned—it's called Black Sun. I've heard Krüger and General Müller, the head of the Gestapo, talking about it. Adolf Hitler is involved."

"Hitler!" Now Tygo had Pieter's interest. "Here?"

"I think so. Krüger has papers in his safe—I can look at them, find out more about it."

"And how do you propose to get into his safe?"

Tygo dug into his pocket and produced the shiny new copy of the safe key.

Pieter glanced at Alisa, who nodded.

"All right, Ferret, go and see what you can find. If it's any use, I'll let you go."

"Thank you," Tygo said.

"But the girl stays here till you get back."

Tygo frowned, but he knew there was nothing he could do. "All right, agreed." He crossed to Willa. "I'll be back as quick as I can."

Willa nodded and, to his surprise, quickly kissed him on the cheek.

"What was that for?" Tygo said. He felt himself blush, and Alisa laughed.

Willa looked a bit awkward now. "Why do you care?" she said. "You're not my boyfriend."

The light was beginning to fade in the sky as Tygo left the printing works on his bicycle. *It must be almost four o'clock*, he thought as he pedaled furiously through the deserted streets. A nearby clock tower confirmed that by striking the hour, and he made it back to HQ pretty fast, only being stopped twice and asked to produce his Gestapo warrant disk to Dutch and German police patrols. Tygo could see they were becoming more nervous, their tempers shorter. Since the New Year he felt an underlying anxiety running through the city. Everyone knew the end was near. The south of the country, beyond Antwerp, had been liberated since Christmas.

Once inside the headquarters, he sprinted up to the third floor and along the corridor to Krüger's corner office. He hadn't quite worked out what he would do if Krüger was there, but luck was finally on his side: The corridor was empty and the office was dark. Perhaps Krüger was down in the cafeteria, or resting after the rigors of the Barcelona trip and all the extra work of the last few days.

Tygo tried the office door. It was locked. He was carrying his set of picks as always, but his heart was going a mile a minute. He had the door open, and then closed and relocked from the inside, in a trice. He was behind Krüger's desk just as quickly, slotting his copied key into the safe. He took a deep breath and twisted it.

The lock flicked back and he turned the handle, sliding the bolt clear. He looked inside: There was the pouch of diamonds, some small ingots of gold, a large bag of gold sovereigns, and lots of documents and certificates. Tygo quickly shuffled through them until he found what he was looking for. Right in the middle of the paper pile was a slim manila folder with the Reich's eagle on it, and the German words for "Black Sun": *Schwarze Sonne*. Next to that were printed the words ABOVE TOP SECRET. This was the information he wanted.

Tygo took the file and opened it on Krüger's desk. Inside were a series of typed sheets. He scanned the pages as fast as he could, his heart pounding. If Krüger caught him now, no amount of excuses or pleading would save his skin. Tygo flicked to the last page, a Teletyped message on thin tissue-like paper.

Tygo stared at it, his heart slamming in his chest. It was a flight order of some sort; Tygo could understand that much. Something to do with the *geheime Flug* he'd overheard General Müller mention. He looked at the bottom; the order was signed by Müller himself. There were two numbered sections. The first one read:

Der Führer und seine Begleitung verlässt dem Flugplatz
52–37 Nord 4–53 Ost
Um 00:00 Uhr 1/14/45—Endziel Barcelona

The second section appeared to be a passenger list:

Hierzu befinden sich in der Begleitung des Führers:

Reichsleiter Bormann
SS-Gruppenführer Müller
SS-Gruppenführer Stumpfegger
SS-Gruppenführer Fegelein
Frau E. Braun
Frau G. Fegelein
6-Mann Begleitkdo RSD
Oberst Krüger

There it was, in black and white, a flight at midnight the next day with the Führer listed as a passenger. Not only him, but Bormann too—Tygo had heard of him and knew he was very important. Krüger must have added his own name; it was handwritten.

He wondered where the coordinates could be. They must be close to Amsterdam if the flight was the next day—probably Schiphol, from where they had flown last night.

Tygo closed the file and tried to deal with the enormity of what he'd discovered. Slowly it began to sink in: the Führer was leaving the next day. He was going to fly to Barcelona from Amsterdam, and then escape from Europe—most probably, he realized, to Buenos Aires in Argentina, with the help of that rich woman Eva Duarte.

He scanned the rest of the file again, searching for more information. Another flight, he saw, was arriving at the same coordinates the next night: *52–37 Nord 4–53 Ost*. But this plane's cargo was listed as just two items: *T-Waffe V6* and *Ur 234 Spezielle Formul.* So was the plane to Barcelona going to carry these as well? What were they?

Tygo stared at the words. *Waffe* meant "weapon," he knew that, and *Ur*—that was some sort of element, wasn't it? He remembered his periodic table from chemistry: Ur stood for uranium. It was radioactive; they had learned about it, and about Marie Curie, in school. And here, it had the words "special formula" after it.

Together they had to be some sort of secret weapon, like the sort that Propaganda Minister Goebbels talked about in his radio broadcast. A weapon that could win the war decisively. What could uranium do to cause such destruction?

Tygo checked through the rest of the papers. Behind that order was another one; it was stamped *"Kriegsmarine"* and had the signature of an admiral called Dönitz at the bottom. It listed a U-2511 submarine, and next to it a place, Cádiz, which Tygo knew was in Spain. There was a long list of personnel and equipment as part of the submarine manifest. There it was again: *Ur 234 Spezielle Formul.* He jotted it down. So the weapon was going to be taken from the Barcelona plane and transported onto the submarine at Cádiz—but where then? To Argentina, with the Führer? It all seemed so far-fetched.

Suddenly Tygo heard footsteps in the corridor. He closed the folder and put it back in the safe, his heart hammering. He got the safe shut and locked, then sprinted to the window. It was too late to get out by the door, and there was nowhere to hide; it would have to be the window.

He slipped behind the long blackout blind and got the window open, then clambered onto the windowsill and stepped out onto the ledge outside. He didn't look down, but pressed himself against the side of the building, shrouded by the darkness. With his right hand he pushed the window closed as far as he could.

He heard Krüger's door slam shut. The wind caught the window and swung it open, fluttering the blackout blind. Tygo heard footsteps and edged as far as he could toward the end of the window ledge. He looked down and saw Krüger's arm reach out to pull the window shut, then heard him lock it.

So now he was stuck. He had planned on waiting for Krüger to leave his office and then climbing back inside. Instead he was standing on a twelve-inch stone ledge three floors above the ground in the dark. And it was beginning to snow.

He glanced down. A wave of dizziness rolled through him, and he pressed himself back against the brickwork again. He looked to his left. Krüger's office was a corner one, and the end of the building was about three yards away. At the apex the gutters joined a heavy iron downpipe that ran all the way down the side of the building to the ground. It was a lifeline, perhaps—or more likely a death warrant. But then, what were his other options? Knock on the window and ask Krüger to let him back in, or leap thirty yards to the rock-hard ground below. No, it was the drainpipe or the final option—freeze to death on the ledge.

Slowly Tygo took off his belt and wrapped the buckle end around his right hand. If he reached the drainpipe he would try to loop the belt around the pipe, thereby giving himself some form of brake to control his slide down it. It meant he would have to leap out and spin in the air so he was facing the brickwork. Could a ferret do it? Probably not, but what choice did he have?

He took a few breaths, then realized he would be better off without his thick overcoat. He unbuttoned it and eased himself out of the sleeves, letting it fall. He took another few breaths, trying to visualize the maneuver he was about to attempt. Every nook, every cranny, every chimney he'd had to climb, every rooftop he'd scrambled over . . . they were nothing compared to what he had to pull off now.

Tygo took one long final breath, held it for a moment, then bent his knees and pushed off from the building with all his strength. He twisted as he fell, and then in an instant he had hit the drainpipe. He lashed the belt around the pipe with his hands and clamped his legs around it. He was sliding down it so fast, and he had to slow himself down. Letting go with his thighs, he pushed his shoulders back, jamming his boots into the wall and kicking at the brickwork to try to slow his descent. Gradually Tygo began to get control, and then his belt slammed into the drainpipe's iron support bracket, the belt was whipped out of his left hand, and he was in free fall. He hit the ground hard, rolling to one side and banging the side of his head.

He lay there in the freezing snow, breathing heavily, and let the pain wash through him. His bullet wound was burning again; the bleeding had probably restarted. He moved his limbs one by one; nothing seemed to be broken. Gingerly he pulled himself to his feet and looked around for his overcoat.

It was a couple of yards away. He picked it up and hobbled stiffly away from the building.

He prayed that the information about Hitler he had would buy him and Willa freedom from the Resistance. The other stuff about the weapon he didn't properly understand. But he put it to the back of his mind for now.

First he had to worry about Krüger.

Always Krüger.

17

The little trio of musicians heralded his arrival back at Resistance headquarters with a spirited rendition of "All the Little Ducklings." Tygo banged on the door to the printing works, feeling keyed-up and expectant. A plan had started to form in his mind as he had ridden there.

The panel in the door slid back, as it had before. "Fred."

"It's me, Tygo . . . is it 'Crosby'?"

"No."

"Please, for God's sake—it's me, you idiot!"

He heard a bolt slide back, and then the door was opened and the same man as before let him in.

"It's 'Ginger,'" the man said peevishly.

Tygo just pushed past him and ran on. He pelted up the stairs to the line of offices and barged into Pieter's office. Pieter and his sister were alone, seated around his desk. Tygo glanced at them; his sister's face was a little flushed. It looked a bit like she had been laughing, or crying; Tygo didn't have time to find out which.

"I've got the information. Where's Willa?" he said.

"Next door," said Alisa, and went to fetch her.

"All right . . . well, it's pretty incredible," Tygo said to Pieter, when Alisa and Willa returned. "If I tell you, will you let me and Willa go?"

"Let's hear it first."

"No, you give me your word," Tygo insisted.

Pieter rolled his tongue over his tobacco-stained teeth. "The word of a free Dutchman? Yes, you have my word."

"It's definitely happening—they're going to fly the Führer out on a plane tomorrow night from here. Amsterdam. I saw the flight orders, signed by General Müller."

Alisa and Pieter were staring at each other.

"Where are they flying from?"

Tygo hesitated for a moment; he had seen the map coordinates on the order but stupidly hadn't written them down—there had been no time. Still, it must be the city airport.

"I don't know, but it's got to be around here—out at Schiphol?"

"Okay. We'll make some inquiries, but if I find out this is all a flight of your imagination, you'll regret it, sonny."

"You won't," Tygo said firmly.

"Well then, you two, what are you waiting for? Off you go, and let us hope our paths never cross again."

Tygo couldn't quite believe it. "You're letting us go?"

"Go on, before I change my mind."

Tygo hugged his sister briefly. "Thank you for everything, Alisa."

"Where are you going?" she asked.

Tygo suddenly felt defensive. "That's none of your business . . . we had an agreement."

"Perhaps so, but Willa has a right to know where you're taking her."

Alisa would always be his big sister, Tygo thought angrily. Protective but controlling. Tygo looked at Willa, then at Pieter, who nodded his agreement.

"Look, it's complicated, all right?" He realized it sounded weak, hollow, childish even.

"Your sister is right. Willa is safe here with us. She has a right to know if you are putting her in danger," Pieter chipped in.

Tygo stood there like a man in the dock with lawyers firing questions at him. They were right, though—what was he thinking? Willa knew nothing about the stone, she had told him so. What could they hope to achieve in the next few hours?

It was time for Tygo to face reality and hope that Krüger would somehow find it in his heart to show mercy. But he had to ask one last time.

"The Red Queen, Willa—do you really know nothing about it? I have to get it to Krüger by midnight."

Willa looked at him, her eyes filled with sadness. "I'm so sorry, Tygo. My mother had it at the beginning of the war, but then I never saw it again, and she never spoke of it. It disappeared . . . perhaps she sold it."

"But it's here, I know it—it's somewhere in this city." Even Tygo was starting to be touched by the stone's mystery.

"Oh, Tygo, what can I do? How can I help you?"

At that moment Tygo understood it was all over for him. Pieter might have given him his freedom for now, but finding that stone in all of Amsterdam, in the next five hours, was hopeless. He knew it, and there was nothing Willa could do either. All he could do was make sure she was safe, and there was only one way to achieve that.

"It's okay, Willa, it's going to be okay." He looked at Alisa and Pieter, who were staring at him. "Willa must stay here with you—you must look after her."

"No!" Willa cried.

Tygo's voice was hoarse. "Trust me, Willa, everything will turn out all right."

But she couldn't meet his eye.

He turned and ran, through the building, out into the night. He ran and ran until he could run no farther, and then he sat down in the snow and wept.

———

Tygo waited until the last minute, just before midnight, when he knew he could not put off meeting Krüger any longer. He had thought about hiding out, trying to get away, running back to his sister, but he knew that with Krüger there was no escape. Perhaps he could lie his way out of it, buy himself a little more time? He was still useful to Krüger. Lie, yes, that was the answer. But deep down, he knew that if Krüger didn't have that stone then he was dead—Müller had said so. And if he was dead so was Tygo.

He walked down the corridor to the office as though it were the plank on a pirate ship. The lights were on and the door was shut. Tygo knocked and waited.

"*Herein,*" came the reply, and Tygo walked in.

Krüger was behind his desk, but the typewriter had been replaced with his velvet pouch of diamonds. He had poured them out over the blotter, and there they sat, a tiny glittering mountain of plundered wealth.

Krüger was wearing a jeweler's loupe in his right eye and examining one of the stones with metal tweezers under his desk lamp. "Four-carat, D color, flawless," he said, placing the stone to one side and selecting another to examine. "What do you think that is worth, Frettchen?"

"I don't know, sir."

"No, I don't suppose you do. Have you returned empty-handed for me?"

Tygo hung his head miserably. "I'm sorry, sir."

"No girl, no Red Queen?" Krüger asked quietly, and Tygo shook his head. "Oh dear, what a shame." A cold, distant tone had seeped into his voice. "No future."

Tygo took a breath. He would go down fighting to the very end.

"The girl died before she could take me to it. She knew where it was."

"What?" That took Krüger by surprise.

"Drowned, sir, in the Amstel canal. We were escaping the Resistance along the towpath, and she slipped on the ice in the dark and went over the side. The ice was thin there. She went under . . . I tried to reach her with a boat hook, but it was too late. I think she was leading me back to the villa." Tygo stopped before he could overdo it.

Krüger stared at him. "The villa? *The villa?* Is that the best you can do?"

"I'm sorry, sir," said Tygo, trying to sound as penitent as he could.

"You know, I'm sorry too. Everything was going so well— my future was very bright, exceptionally bright." He held up one of the stones; it flashed like the lamp in a lighthouse. "Here, look . . ."

Tygo walked to the desk and stared at the pile of diamonds. A king's ransom, but nothing to the Red Queen, he thought. One stone that could determine so many people's destinies.

"One would be a fool, as head of the plunder squad, not to make some financial provision for the future. And I am not a fool, Tygo. Let us hope it is enough to provide me with a little house somewhere warm, if not the estate I was hoping for," Krüger said, starting to scoop the diamonds back into the velvet pouch. He turned to the open safe and placed the pouch inside. "What were you hoping for, Frettchen? That I would be merciful?"

Tygo nodded.

"Under the circumstances, seeing that you are about to lose me my passage to Argentina and I must make other plans, I am afraid I am not inclined to clemency—despite the fact that, believe it or not, I have become quite fond of you."

Which is a long-winded way of saying you're going to kill me, thought Tygo. He dropped his head.

"We still have till tomorrow to find it, sir. Give me another chance."

"I'm sorry, you've had that already."

Tygo nodded, accepting his fate. It was then that he heard the sound of footsteps in the corridor, boots running toward the office. Krüger's eyes widened in surprise and Tygo spun around.

"What is the meaning of this?" said Krüger.

"She insisted on seeing you, sir!" the young soldier blustered.

Willa was standing in the doorway, her cheeks pink from exertion. She was breathing hard. Tygo stared at her, slack-jawed.

"Drowned?" Krüger was looking at him.

"Sir, I . . . uh . . . she must have gotten out of the water . . ."

Krüger strode past him. "Dismissed, sergeant." He took hold of Willa's arm and led her into the room.

"She's bone dry, you little liar. Is this some sort of joke, Frettchen?"

"A joke?" Tygo echoed weakly. Yes, he thought, it was in a way—an enormous cosmic joke that he couldn't begin to get his head around.

"Yes, a joke, Herr Oberst. That's it," said Tygo.

"It would seem luck is with you once again, if only for a little while. For some reason she has come of her own accord." He glanced at Tygo, and then at Willa, trying to figure out why. "No, surely not. What do we have here? Young love? Good grief, how touching."

Willa came to Tygo's side. Suddenly the phone on Krüger's desk rang. Krüger crossed to it.

"Krüger." He listened for a moment. "General Müller, I have been meaning to report . . ." He covered the mouthpiece. "Outside, wait for me outside!"

Tygo and Willa closed the door and sat down on the leather couch in the corridor.

"You came back, Willa . . ." Tygo began.

"Shut up and listen, Tygo. We haven't got much time. I think I know where the stone is."

"What?"

"After you left, I remembered something Mother did at Christmas the night before she died. Maybe she knew it was too late for her." Willa slipped off the gold locket that hung around her neck on a piece of ribbon. "She gave me this." She opened the locket. Inside there was a black-and-white photo of a baby.

"You?"

Willa nodded. "She made me promise never to lose it. She said it held the two most precious things she had in the world. At the time I didn't really take any notice of that. But then tonight, when you asked about the stone, it made me think again." She glanced up and down the corridor. "Look!"

She slipped her fingernail under the photo and eased it out. Beneath it was a piece of paper folded into a tight square. She quickly unfolded it for Tygo's inspection.

"It's a ticket receipt to a shop in the city. Look, it has a number on it, and the name and address. If you can find it, I believe you will find the stone."

Tygo stared at her. If she was right, there was still a chance—more than a chance—but he had to go now. Right now. He took her hand.

"Come on."

Willa shook her head. "No, if we both just disappear he'll think we've gone on the run, send his men to find us—and when they do, they'll take the stone."

Tygo's mind was racing. She was right—Krüger was becoming more desperate and unpredictable as the hours ticked down. Better he got the stone and then engineered the right circumstances to negotiate with him.

"Are you sure, Willa?"

She nodded.

"Tell Krüger I've gone to get the stone. Tell him if he touches a hair on your head he'll never see the stone, or me, again. Trust me, he needs it—his life depends on it."

"I'll tell him," Willa said.

Tygo looked at her. He needed to get away, but he also needed to ask her something.

"Why did you do this? Come back for me?"

Willa stared back at him. "You did a brave thing for me tonight, Tygo. You didn't have to, but you did anyway. I just felt it was the right thing to do."

"Thank you," Tygo said, and this time he leaned forward to kiss her softly on the cheek.

18

It took Tygo a lot longer than he would have liked to find the shop. He had to show his Gestapo warrant disk and letter four times to get through the checkpoints that ringed the inner city, but finally he located it in a side street, its metal shutters pulled firmly down and padlocked. The front door was also locked. He banged on it with his fist and pulled the bell stop, but no one came.

Tygo set to work and quickly picked the mortise, but he still couldn't get the door open. The proprietor had lodged a metal bar into the floor and set it against the inside of the door. He would need a sledgehammer to take out the hinges if he wanted to get in that way.

Tygo stepped back and took stock. It was a two-story building, like his family's shop, probably with accommodation on the upper floor. It had the traditional crow-stepped gable on the front. Tygo knew he had only one option left: climb onto the roof and hope there was a skylight to get in through.

The cast-iron drainpipe was agonizingly cold on his hands as he pulled himself up the side of the building. At last he reached the stepped gable and carefully climbed up it to the top, where the roof ridge ran away to the back of the building. Sure enough, there was a skylight about a few feet down each side of the roof, but both were latched closed. Tygo straddled the roof ridge and shimmied along it until he was level with the windows. What could he do? Again, his choice was limited.

He swung his leg over so that he was sitting perched on the top of the roof ridge, the window just below his outstretched legs. He would need to spring forward and hit the glass pane with his boots, falling through it and hopefully not breaking his neck. If he missed, he was down the icy roof and over the side to the street below in an instant.

Tygo rocked his upper body, his hands pressing into the ridge tiles, his heels pressed against the roof. He took a deep breath and sprang forward with all his strength. His boots hit the glass together. It shattered into fat pieces and he fell through, hitting the floor below and rolling to one side, then slamming into something hard.

Tygo glanced up. It was a heavy wardrobe, and in the gloom he could make out a single bed and a washstand with basin and jug. He got to his feet, a little unsteadily, and brushed himself down. His bullet wound throbbed. He peered around and saw a single brass candlestick on the bedside table, with an inch of candle still in it. Tygo found his matches and lit it. It gave a weak, jaundiced pool of light, but it was enough for him to make his way downstairs.

"Is there anyone here?" he called out softly, the stairs creaking under his feet. There came no reply. When he reached the bottom of the stairs he stepped into a narrow corridor. The inside of the shop was through a door in the middle. Tygo stepped inside and shone the candle ahead. Then he screamed and jumped back, tripping and falling onto his bottom. An enormous polar bear was standing in front of him, its massive-clawed paws outstretched and ready to strike, its mouth with long, yellow fangs open and ready.

Tygo stared at it for a moment, his heart racing, then glanced around. On all sides glass cases and cabinets were stacked, filled with all kinds of animals: birds, dogs, foxes, rabbits, eagles, even a crocodile. Tygo got to his feet. It was a taxidermist's shop, and the polar bear was the prize exhibit, standing—he could see now—on a plinth that resembled a huge block of ice. The owner had even put a swastika armband around its right arm, which—now he came to think of it—actually looked like the bear was making the Nazi salute. It made him smile, and he wondered what its name was—Peppy, maybe, like the mascot for the mint candies?

After taking in his surroundings for a moment, Tygo set to work. He had to find the ledger book that held the counterpart to Willa's receipt. There was a tall counter running along the end wall of the shop, and Tygo discovered a large brass lantern on it with some oil still inside. He lit it with the last of his guttering candle; that improved things a great deal. He stepped around the counter and, for the second time in a minute, his heart missed a beat.

In front of him, slumped in a battered striped deck chair, was an old man, covered in furs top to bottom, from his racoon hat to his bearskin boots. His eyes were closed, a thin layer of frost covered his furs, and tiny icicles dropped down from his bushy, unkempt eyebrows.

Tygo edged forward and prodded him with his finger. He felt rock hard. He touched the man's cheek with the back of his hand; it was stone cold. Dead as a doornail.

Tygo blew on his hands and rubbed them together. It was truly as cold as a morgue in this shop that was filled to the brim with dead things. He shivered, set the lamp down, and started to work his way through the drawers beneath the counter until he found what he was looking for: a small workbook with the original tickets on one side and a carbon copy beneath the top page. He flicked through it until he found the matching order number: 27. There was no description on the order.

Tygo looked around. He couldn't see anything with that number on it, but it had to be here. He made his way back through the shop between the bell jars and glass boxes, their contents staring at him with their glass eyes. Then he saw a large shelved cabinet running the full length of the wall at the other end of the shop. It was full of brown paper packages tied up with string, neatly stacked on its glass shelves. They were of varying sizes, but each one, Tygo could see as soon as he'd opened the cabinet, had a small label attached to it, bearing a number.

Tygo worked his way through the packages, finding every number but 27. Once he'd checked the lower shelves he had to stop and hunt around until he found a set of steps so he could reach the higher ones. He worked on, moving along the shelves and climbing back up. A feeling of panic was setting in.

"It has to be here. It *has* to be here!"

Tygo realized he was shouting the words aloud at the top of his voice. His hands had started shaking. Only three more packages remained: 102 . . . 19 . . . he tossed them aside, grasping the last one, which was small—no bigger than a box of cook's matches. He looked at the ticket: 27.

Twenty-seven.

He threw his head back and yelled out in relief. The action saved his life: At that very instant he felt a searing pain against his left ear, as if someone had stuck a red-hot needle through it. The glass in the cabinet exploded in his face, and he toppled back off the stepladder to the floor as the sound of the gunshot filled the room.

Tygo scrambled to his feet, a trickle of blood running down his neck, still clutching the package in his hand.

Another gunshot, the bullet smacking into the wall just to his left.

He grabbed the oil lamp and just had time to glimpse the other end of the shop before a bullet hit the lamp and ripped it out of his hand, leaving him with just the wire handle. But that was all the time Tygo needed to realize he had to get the hell out of the shop right this second. The man he'd thought was dead was standing behind the counter with some ancient bolt-action rifle in his hand.

"You thieving little . . ."

The frozen voice bellowed out in the gloom.

Tygo ran toward the front door, barging into glass cabinets and sending them crashing to the floor. Another bullet sang past him and blew the head off a large blue parrot perching on a tropical branch.

Tygo heard the man reloading as he reached the front door, pulled the metal bar away, and slid back the bolts. His neck was wet with blood. Then he had the door open and was out into the street, running as fast as he could as the man's angry cries faded.

19

The sound of the heavy bomber woke Krüger. After Tygo had left, he had made his way out to the secret air base on the coast as per his orders, bringing the girl with him. He was to remain there until evening, when the Führer and his party would arrive. But first the secret shipment was due to arrive from Peenemünde, and that was the bomber now, circling, trying to land.

Krüger hurried out from his tent, buttoning his leather greatcoat, the deep throbbing of the engines above him, almost on top of him. The canvas on the outside of the tent was white with frost, and he was chilled to the marrow. He stared up at the dawn sky, checking his watch. Just before five; he'd managed a couple of hours' sleep.

He made his way through the gloom toward the temporary airstrip, which the engineers had constructed where the forest gave way to sandy dunes. He could hear the surf, and the air had a salty tang to it. Krüger nodded to the guard standing outside another tent, close to a cluster of vehicles: support trucks, a radio truck, field kitchen, and an ambulance.

"The girl?"

"Secure, sir."

Krüger reached the edge of the airstrip. Sections of steel strips lay on the leveled ground, a series of drums filled with fuel were burning brightly along its perimeter, and someone had lit flares down its center line. The bomber had dropped through the low clouds and was thundering toward Krüger, its landing lights blazing. It touched down with a great thump, lifted up again for a moment, then settled, barreling toward him. *It's never going to stop in time*, he thought, and turned to run—then, with a great whoosh, a large parachute deployed from the rear gun turret and the plane shuddered violently as it slowed right down. When it finally came to a halt, the pilot swung the bomber around so that it was already lined up for a quick exit.

A team of Luftwaffe service personnel hurried past Krüger to begin unloading its cargo. Satisfied all was in order, Krüger turned and walked back into the trees until he reached a small clearing, in the center of which was another transport plane. Camouflage netting had been strung above it.

It was one of the few remaining Arado heavy transport planes that were still serviceable. It looked a bit like the

Liberator that had taken him to Barcelona, with a high wing above the fuselage and four beefy engines. But its tail was different; it had a long pontoon from the wing to the double tail at the back. This meant that the fuselage itself, which was fat and stubby, actually ended just past the front wing. Krüger made his way to it and found that the doors had been folded back and a ramp lowered to allow easy loading. Inside was a cavernous space.

Now Krüger was close up, he noticed the strange undercarriage. In addition to the normal three-wheel tricycle arrangement, it also had two neat rows of smaller wheels along the bottom of the fuselage. It was an amazing-looking craft, he thought.

Krüger decided to take a look inside while he waited for the cargo to arrive from the other plane. He walked up the ramp and stared at the open cargo area. It was completely open right up to the cockpit, except for a compartment on the right-hand side. He walked down toward it. Several metal seats had been bolted in pairs down the side of the fuselage before one reached the compartment, and other equipment was attached to the side, including fire extinguishers and a metal ax. The compartment had clearly been specially fabricated and fitted inside the plane; there were scorch marks to the metal where the welds had been made.

Krüger carefully opened the door to the compartment. This was to be for the Führer's exclusive use. It was surprisingly spacious and had been furnished like a sitting room, with wicker armchairs bolted to the floor, a daybed along one wall, and a table and a set of chairs next to it. A copy of Hitler's favorite portrait of Frederick the Great had been screwed to a wall in a metal frame. There was even a cold box for food and drink. Krüger closed the door and made his way back down the plane, mentally selecting a suitable seat for himself.

A few moments later the ground crew appeared through the darkness, with two tracked vehicles being driven at a walking pace. This type of vehicle was known as the Kettenkrad and consisted of a motorbike at the front with a set of tracks behind it, perfect for pulling heavy loads.

The first one spun around when it reached the bottom of the ramp, and then reversed slowly up, its tracks smacking on the metal.

Strapped to it was a rocket—an A-4B, about five yards in length with a smooth conical nose, a three-foot-long needle at its tip. In the middle of the rocket were two winglets, and at the end, four long fins. A fat rocket exhaust cone sat beneath them. It was lashed to a wooden pallet that had bright yellow buoyancy bags fitted all around, with CO_2 cylinders to inflate them.

Krüger watched as it was carefully unloaded from the Kettenkrad and secured to the floor of the cargo hold. The Kettenkrad rolled back down the ramp, and the second one reversed up.

This one was carrying a wooden crate about the size of a tea chest, which the men unloaded very carefully. Krüger was not surprised—next to the Reich's eagle, together with the serial numbers from Krüger's file, was stamped in large letters: GEFAHR DES TODES. NICHT ÖFFNEN.

Danger of Death. Do Not Open.

So Müller had been telling him the truth. This was the wonder weapon that would soon attack New York and win them the war.

"I want a permanent guard around this plane from now till takeoff," he said. "Ten men—six outside, four inside."

"Yes, Herr Oberst." A sergeant saluted him.

He turned at the sound of a girl's cry and saw Willa being manhandled by a soldier at the front of the cargo plane.

"Bring her here!" he barked, and the soldier led her down toward him. Krüger pointed to the inside of the plane.

"Take a good look, you foolish child."

Willa craned her neck and stared into the plane.

"What do you see?"

Willa shrugged. "Some sort of rocket."

"You have just seen the future. A single weapon that has the power to obliterate an entire city."

"I don't believe you," said Willa.

"*Ja*, I know." Krüger smiled. "I don't believe it either, but fifty years ago, no one would have believed we could fly in such huge machines such as these." He touched the side of the ramp, then started to walk back toward the main camp. Willa followed him. "Perhaps fifty years from now, we will be doing things no one thought possible. Living on the moon perhaps."

Willa shook her head.

"Why not? With these weapons we will win the war, and then with our technology we will transform it." Krüger glanced at her. "So you had better hope Frettchen soon appears with that stone, if you are to have any chance of seeing that day."

"What about you?" Willa said, almost contemptuously.

He dismissed her with a wave of his hand. But in fact, she was right: The Führer had promised the stone to the Duarte woman. If Krüger couldn't produce it, he was finished.

"Take her back to my tent, and if she escapes again I will have the guard shot."

20

General Müller was finally feeling human again. Having arrived at the Adlerhorst early in the morning, he had managed five hours of sleep. Upon rising he had enjoyed a hot bath—the first in days—and a good shave from Bormann's valet, and was now wearing a fresh uniform. He had just finished his excellent breakfast of ham and eggs, and was walking across the castle courtyard with a swing in his step and a smile on his face. Müller was not one to smile—ever—but today he treated himself to an approximation of one. He felt optimistic; everything was going according to the plan and was on time. How very German.

Even the weather was good, with some rays of sunshine that bode very well for their departure to Zandvoort at nine o'clock. The only fly in the ointment remained the Führer's chronic indecision. He had changed his mind at least a dozen times in the last two days, from agreeing to the plan to believing a return to the bunker in Berlin was the better option. Müller had left Bormann to work on him with his subtle persuasive skills.

Müller reached the radio room and composed a short message to Oberst Krüger, advising him of their expected departure and arrival time and requesting confirmation that everything was ready at the airfield. He handed the message to the operator, who quickly encoded it and sent it out on the Enigma machine. Then he sat and smoked a cigarette while he waited for the reply, which duly arrived. Excellent—the cargo had arrived safely, but, Müller noted, there was no mention of the Red Queen.

Müller walked back across the castle courtyard to call on Bormann and to check the time of departure. He stopped to make a final inspection of the vehicles waiting there; as with the airstrip engineers, he had had to twist arms in order to put together a secure convoy.

For the sake of speed and secrecy, he had ruled out using the Führer's armored train and had instead found the fastest armored cars available. These were Pumas fitted with Porsche engines—one with flak guns, one with a double cannon, and one with radio capability. They could reach up to thirty miles an hour and were fitted with long-range tanks. There would be two at the front and the flak one at the back. Between the Pumas were two of Hitler's own six-wheeled Mercedes, capable of carrying seven people in comfort and safety. Müller had asked for machine guns to be fitted to the running boards at the front, and had had the tires switched to road ones in order to lift the top speed to that of the armored cars.

Finally, there was a fuel truck, a mechanical support truck, a field ambulance, and a transport with a platoon of the Führer's own Leibstandarte SS troops.

He turned from his inspection and found that Bormann was coming to meet him. It was hard to tell if he was smiling or experiencing an attack of indigestion. Müller hoped it was the former.

"Good news?" Müller asked.

"Not for me, I feel like my stomach is on fire." He rubbed his stomach with his gloved hand.

"Has the Führer made his decision?"

"He is conducting the morning briefing with the OKW now, reviewing the position on the Western Front. I will ask him for a decision as soon as that meeting finishes."

The two men stood in the snow for a few minutes, each lost in his own thoughts. Then the door to the Führer's hut opened and a series of army generals started to drift out with their adjutants. They all looked tired and dispirited.

"We cannot hold this operation beyond tonight, you know that," said Müller quietly. "Either we leave or we stand it down."

"Don't tell me my business," snapped Bormann. "I will speak to him. Wait here."

He pushed through the thinning crowd and disappeared inside. Müller lit a cigarette and glanced around. In the west corner of the courtyard, Eva Braun was standing with her sister, Gretl. The two women were both dressed for the road, in wool skirts and coats, strong walking boots, and fur hats.

Müller thought they looked tense as they chatted together and stamped their feet. Well, if all went to plan, in two weeks they would be wearing cotton dresses and enjoying the warm winter sunshine of Buenos Aires. The Führer would give the final order, and the Type XXI U-boat, which would by then be waiting underwater just off the coast of the United States, would launch the missile that would reduce New York to dust.

After ten minutes Bormann emerged from the hut, wearing the same tight smile on his face.

"Good news?" Müller asked again.

"Not for our boys in the Ardennes."

"It's bad?"

"It's over. Retreating on all fronts, no fuel for the Panzers, no bullets for the infantry. Same in the east—a massive offensive by the Reds, over two million men."

"Well then, surely—"

"Of course the Führer has made the right decision!"

Müller rubbed his gloved hands. "Operation Black Sun is authorized?"

Bormann nodded. "Get the vehicles started and the crews ready," he said. "We leave in thirty minutes."

21

After Tygo had escaped from the taxidermist, he had immediately cycled back to Gestapo Headquarters. On arrival he had been informed that Krüger had left some time ago with Willa, heading for an undisclosed location. He had left a sealed envelope in his office for Tygo.

Tygo had run upstairs to Krüger's office. On his desk was the envelope. Tygo ripped it open and saw that Krüger had written out the coordinates of the airfield. He recognized them: *52–37 Nord 4–53 Ost.* He looked over at the large-scale map on the wall and quickly located the place . . . only there was no sign of an airfield there. It was all woods and dunes on the coast not far from Zandvoort, which had been a holiday resort before the war. The whole area had been out of bounds to civilians since the Occupation. It would take a couple of hours to cycle there, Tygo thought, perhaps a little more.

He sat down at the desk, jotting a route out below the coordinates on the piece of paper. When he had finished he sat there and stared at the paper package from the taxidermist's. What if the stone wasn't inside? What then?

Finally he reached forward and started to open it. He slipped off the string and tore at the paper, revealing a stiff cardboard box. Slowly he took off the lid and stared at the contents.

It was a stuffed field mouse wearing traditional red wooden clogs and a striped sailor's jersey, topped off with a little red pointed Dutch hat.

Tygo held it in his hand for a moment, then gave it a squeeze; he could feel something hard in the mouse's abdomen. He pulled up the jersey and saw an incision from neck to tail. He pulled roughly at the stitching, and out it popped onto the desk in front of him. The Red Queen. Bigger than a gobstopper, a single red diamond. From his work with Krüger, he knew enough to know that red diamonds like this simply did not exist.

"*Unbezahlbar,*" Tygo whispered. Priceless, that was what Krüger had called it. It seemed crazy that something so small could be worth so much, but when he looked at it, it was truly extraordinary.

He picked it up between his thumb and forefinger and held it up to the light. The stone seemed to come alive, to catch fire . . . the most perfect ruby color, iridescent, as dark as pigeon's blood, shooting out blinding little flashes of light.

There existed no other diamond of that size and color in the whole world. And he was sitting in Gestapo Headquarters holding it in his hand. A two-hour cycle ride and Krüger would have it, and he and Willa would be free.

He started to get up, then stared at the typed coordinates again. What about the Resistance, his sister and Pieter? Here was a chance to kill Hitler, maybe even to end the war. Deep down he knew he had to get them this vital information, and as soon as possible.

Getting through the city took Tygo some time; he should have used his skates, he thought. The patrols were out in force, checkpoints had increased, and he could feel that the German field police were getting edgier. He was stopped at least five times and asked for his identity papers. His Gestapo warrant disk and Krüger's letter did the trick every time, though, and he finally got to the printing works around ten.

The drab gray street was deserted except for the three lookout boys, who duly piped and drummed his arrival. Tygo propped his bike by the front entrance and banged on the door.

"Hurry up!" he yelled.

After a moment or two the hatch behind the grille in the door slid back and the same guard's face appeared.

"You again."

"I need to see Pieter." Tygo could feel his temper rising.

"Go away," said the man, but not in such polite language.

"Listen, I have some very important information for him." Tygo leaned forward with his face to the grille.

The other man's face came closer too. "Get lost, sonny."

In a second, Tygo had reached through with his left hand and grabbed the man's scarf, pulling it through the grille and wrapping it around the vertical bar. He pulled it tight, jamming the man's face up against the grille.

The man's face was red. "He's not here," he hissed as he struggled for air.

"What?" said Tygo.

"You heard."

Tygo hadn't been expecting that. He thought for a moment. "What about my sister?"

"They went out together."

The young man's face was going a darker shade of red. Tygo kept up the pressure. "Where?"

Once again the man told Tygo to get lost, his language even more colorful.

Tygo cinched the scarf tighter still. The man's eyes were now bulging in their sockets, his lips blue.

"Blue Windmill café," he just managed to whisper, then his eyes rolled up in his head. Tygo let go of his grip; the scarf loosened and the man promptly disappeared backward and landed with a thump on the floor inside, unconscious.

Tygo knew that café; it had been Alisa's favorite place before the war. But it was on the other side of the Amstel. He turned and ran for his bike.

He stood outside the café for a minute or two. It looked closed: The blackout blinds were down on the front door, and it was shuttered and locked. Tygo took out his leather pouch of picks and selected one. He probed the lock with the snake pin and had the door open in a minute.

The place was empty, really empty. The furniture was gone, the glasses and the bottles were gone, everything was gone. A dog was lying in front of the fireplace. On its back, legs in the air, frozen stiff and almost comically dead.

Tygo looked down at the floor. Sure enough, there were footprints on the boards, where the snow had melted off boots, leading to a spiral staircase at the back.

Tygo knelt down and unlaced his own boots, slipping them off. Had that Resistance fighter been lying? He might have set him up for an ambush. He padded softly over the wooden boards and up the cast-iron grille treads of the staircase. There was a landing at the top of the stairs, with doors leading off it.

Tygo held his breath and listened. He was pretty sure someone was in the end room. He slid along the wall toward it, but halfway there, a floorboard betrayed him with a low squeak as he stepped on it. He lifted his foot off and it squeaked again.

He thought he heard movement from the end door, feet hitting the floor.

He was almost there when the door literally flew at him, coming off its hinges and hitting him full on, slamming him off his feet. He fell straight down on his back, the door on top of him, a tremendous weight on top of that.

"Don't move a muscle," a deep voice growled from behind the door. A painfully familiar one.

"For God's sake!" yelled Tygo. "It's me, Tygo."

He felt the great weight being lifted off him, and then the door was removed and Pieter was standing, staring down at him.

Tygo pulled himself to his feet. "You nearly broke my neck!" he said.

"Next time I will!" Pieter replied. He was dressed in nothing but a pair of woolen trousers held up with suspenders. His barrel chest was a carpet of black hair. He turned and stepped back toward the bedroom. "I thought we agreed never to see each other again."

"We did," said Tygo.

"Then you had better have a good reason for being here, because all that stuff about Hitler wasn't worth a bucket of warm spit."

"Actually, I do, and you're wrong. I've got new . . ." The word "information" died in his mouth.

His sister, Alisa, had appeared in the shattered doorway. He stared at her, then at Pieter.

"You were saying . . ."

"I was saying . . ."

"Why don't we all go downstairs?" his sister said.

Tygo nodded. Was something going on between his sister and Pieter? Surely not.

They stood at the bar, Alisa and Pieter on one side, Tygo on the other. Pieter was like some big gorilla, his fist clamped around the neck of a bottle of Dutch gin. He took a swig and passed it to Tygo, who took a quick sip just to be polite. He coughed and his eyes watered. He was surprised to see his sister take a healthy slug, and he realized all of sudden she looked a lot older than she had last year.

"So don't keep us in suspense. What information do you have?" Pieter cracked his knuckles.

Gorilla, Tygo thought again.

"It's all true," he said, "Hitler is being flown out tonight from here."

"Rubbish. We checked the airports, we've got people on the inside of everything."

"Yes, but I've seen the coordinates—they've built a secret airstrip out at Zandvoort, by the beach. There's a special plane waiting for him. Krüger's taken Willa there. It's going to happen, I swear."

"So she did come to find you," said Alisa.

Tygo nodded. "Don't worry, I'm going to save her."

"Oh, Tygo," Alisa said, and smiled.

"I'm serious."

"I know you are."

Pieter took a final swig, wiping his mouth. "Hitler flying out tonight? I know what I think," he scoffed. "But I'm going to ask your sister what she thinks."

Alisa took Tygo's hand. "Look, Tygo, I know you're in trouble with Krüger, and I know you care about this girl Willa, but if this is some sort of silly story . . ."

"I'm not lying." Tygo was angry, but Alisa was not moved. She stared intently at him.

"If you are, I will kill you," Alisa said very quietly.

"If I am, I will let you."

Alisa looked over to Pieter and nodded.

"Seriously?" Pieter said, then sighed. "All right, let's hear it."

Tygo took a breath and dove in. "Like I said, I have the coordinates, and I've made a plan of the route to it. They're going to fly Hitler out with some other people; I saw a list of their names. They're taking a secret weapon with them. I'm pretty sure they're going to Spain, and then after that to Argentina, probably by submarine. I saw another order signed by a Kriegsmarine admiral called Dönitz."

"You didn't mention that before," Pieter said skeptically.

"Stop it, Pieter!" Alisa snapped.

"Oh, come on, Alisa . . ." replied Pieter.

"He's my brother. I love him and I trust him. If he says that's what's going to happen, then that's what's going to happen."

Tygo was astonished to see Pieter hold up his hands in apology.

"All right, all right, I'm sorry." Pieter looked at Tygo. "Just supposing it's true, what are we supposed to do? Storm the plane? We don't have the people for that, the weapons."

"No, there's a better way," said Tygo. "Do you have a map?"

"Just a minute," Alisa said, and disappeared back upstairs. She returned with a large-scale map, which she spread across the bar.

Tygo pointed out the location of the airstrip. "There's only one road there, through the woods. Look. You have to approach it on the road going south from Haarlem. There's an unmarked turn that goes over a bridge crossing the Northern canal."

"A bridge?"

"Yes, exactly. Don't you have explosives, dynamite?"

"Blow the bridge," said Pieter.

"Ambush the convoy," Alisa chimed in.

"The plane leaves at midnight," said Tygo.

Pieter glanced at Alisa. "It's new moon tonight—it will be dark, good cover for us." He looked at his watch. "It's noon now—we have three hours of daylight, maybe a little more, to get everything ready and in position. It's going to be tight."

"What choice do we have?" said Alisa.

Pieter shrugged and leaned forward, handing the bottle of gin to Tygo.

"You know, Tygo, if this is true—you just might win the war tonight."

Tygo grinned and took a swig. It burned all the way down. He handed it back and turned to leave.

"Where do you think you're going?" his sister asked.

"I have to get back to Willa. I promised." He felt for the Red Queen deep in his pocket.

Alisa shook her head. "I'm sorry, Tygo, we need your help first."

Tygo stared back at his sister, torn. It was the hardest decision he'd ever had to make.

But at last he nodded: Krüger and Willa would have to wait.

22

Tygo knew he couldn't refuse, but he still fretted about Willa, stuck in the clutches of Krüger. If it all went well there would be time, he told himself. Pieter had asked if he could somehow get them some transport, and on his way back to Gestapo HQ he had a brilliant idea that would kill two birds with one stone.

As soon as he was inside the building he hurried to the radio communication room. One of the operators recognized him; Krüger often assigned him the job of bringing down his written messages for transmission.

"Hello, Frettchen, how can I help you today?"

Tygo picked up a message pad and wrote out a short message. "Could you send this to Oberst Krüger, most urgent?"

The operator took the pad. "Message reads: 'Red Queen safe. Request immediate transport order. Signed Frettchen.'"

Tygo nodded.

"It'll be a couple of minutes."

Tygo paced continuously while the radio operator sent the coded signal and they waited for a reply. They did not have to wait long. The operator passed the message across:

"'Request granted. I hereby order the Transport Department to provide immediate use of any available vehicle to Tygo Winter in pursuit of his duties to Oberst Krüger. By order.'"

Tygo hurried down to the basement, where the transport department was. He showed the quartermaster his warrant disk and the order just issued by Krüger. Normally the quartermaster would have told him where to go—cars and gasoline were in short supply—but Tygo was in no mood for this.

"Contact him yourself, if you doubt me," he said.

Instead, the quartermaster picked up the phone and called Günter, Krüger's driver. What the hell—they could take his Opel.

Tygo ordered Günter to stop Krüger's car a sensible distance from the printing works so as not arouse the itchy trigger finger of the guard at the door. Tygo knew he didn't need much of a reason to shoot him; that was also why he'd taken the precaution, when they had stopped, of removing the P38 service revolver from the holster attached to the inside of the front passenger door.

"Wait here," he said, enjoying giving orders rather than taking them. He got out of the car and slotted the revolver into the back of his trousers. It was like a cold stone at the bottom of his spine.

Tygo jogged to the front of the works. He knocked. The same face appeared.

"Hello again."

There was no reply; the young man just opened the door. *But if looks could kill*, thought Tygo, pushing past him.

He stood at the back as Pieter briefed a group of about thirty women and men, mostly in their twenties, Tygo guessed. To his surprise Ursula and the two boys were there too.

"What are they doing here?"

Alisa glanced over at them for a moment. "Pieter thinks we need every single person we can get our hands on—that convoy is going to be very well armed. We could lose a lot of people."

Tygo listened, finally realizing what a deadly undertaking was being planned. So did the others, he could see that too. Steely faces, determined, listening intently as Pieter assigned each of them their own task in the ambush. All except Ursula, who stuck her tongue out at Tygo when he caught her eye. It made him grin; perhaps they would have stayed friends if things had been different for him and his family.

Alisa was standing beside him, and Tygo could see from the way she glanced at Pieter that there was something between them. He realized he was beginning to feel a bit like that about Willa. The briefing was drawing to a close. Pieter and Alisa had agreed beforehand not to tell the other members who the target was, but only to say that it was a very high-ranking member of the German army.

"Any questions?" Pieter asked.

There were a few murmurs, but everyone seemed to know what they had to do. The briefing broke up and most people hurried from the building. Time was short.

"See you out there, Frettchen." It was Ursula, her two side-kicks beside her.

"Can we call a truce, Ursula?"

She looked at him. "I have neither the time nor the inclination," she said pompously, and pushed past.

Tygo shook his head and hurried over to his sister. "You ready?" he asked, anxious to be on his way to the airbase.

"Yes, but we need you to take out the driver. After that we'll take the car, and you'll have to get us through any checkpoints, to the arms dump at Haarlem. We can load what we need from there and bring it to the bridge."

"After that, you can do what you like," Pieter added.

Tygo felt a surge of relief. The Red Queen was burning a hole in his pocket.

Günter never saw it coming. With a cheery greeting, Tygo clambered into the back of the car, wearing brass knuckle-dusters that Pieter had loaned him for the purpose, and hit him just behind his left ear. Günter slumped forward over the wheel, unconscious, the horn blaring momentarily till Tygo could haul him back off it.

Pieter opened the driver's door, and together they bundled the comatose soldier into the printing works. Once inside they stripped him of his uniform and left him tied up, watched over by a Resistance guard who had stayed behind. Pieter pulled on the driver's uniform. It just managed to fit, although the sleeves were too short. He jammed the gray forage cap on.

"Quickly now, we need to make a couple of stops in the city."

The three of them hurried out, Tygo taking the trouble to relock the door. Out in the street, Alisa climbed into the trunk while Tygo and Pieter got into the front seats. Pieter started the car, and they were away.

They drove out through the city slowly and cautiously. They were almost clear when they ran into a mobile checkpoint: A field police Kübelwagen had been placed across the road. Pieter slowed the vehicle.

"Checkpoint!" he shouted back to Alisa. She had a Sten gun in the boot with her, and she would cock it now.

"Where are you going?" the military policeman asked, leaning in.

"I have orders here from Oberst Krüger." Tygo handed the man the letter Krüger had written him, together with his Gestapo warrant disk.

The man studied them, then looked inside the car. Tygo sat still, staring straight ahead.

"Where are you going?" the man repeated, handing the papers back.

"My destination is secret. If you wish to contact Oberst Krüger's office they will be happy to confirm that." Tygo's heart was going *thump, thump, thump*.

The other police officer was walking around the car, his submachine gun pointed at them. "This is Oberst Krüger's car, *ja*?" he said.

Tygo nodded. "I am acting under his orders, like I said."

"Then where is Günter?"

It was just Tygo's bad luck to run into a policeman who actually knew Krüger's driver.

"He's sick today; this is Klaus, his replacement."

Pieter nodded to the men. The lead policeman looked at his colleague, who shrugged.

"All right, on your way."

Pieter put the car into gear and they pulled away. Tygo looked in the rearview mirror; the two policemen were staring after them.

They drove on without meeting any further patrols or checkpoints. After a short while, they were passing through the outskirts of Haarlem and then back into the countryside, overtaking the occasional cyclist and pedestrian as they struggled with carts filled with foraged kindling. The countryside had been picked clean of anything that could be eaten or burned, and the rest was covered in snow and ice.

Pieter made a right turn up a farm track and the Opel bounced and bumped over the rutted frozen mud, the wheels spinning until Pieter dropped the car into a lower gear. At the end of the track was an abandoned farmhouse, brick-built with traditional Dutch gables. A windmill was behind it, bereft of its wooden slat sails, long ago taken for firewood. It made for an excellent hiding place, and it had not taken them long to reach it. Time was still on their side.

They all climbed out of the car, Alisa stretching out her freezing, cramped body. She kept the Sten gun slung over her shoulder. Tygo stamped on a frozen puddle with his boot. It made a star-shaped little crater like a bullet hole.

"Let's be quick about this." Pieter led them into the farmhouse. The sun was low in the sky and it was gloomy inside. They stood in the hallway for a moment, then walked through into the kitchen. "The cellar is through the pantry—you go back and keep a lookout in the hall, Tygo. Your sister and I will get the stuff."

Tygo nodded and walked back into the hall. He rested his hand on the butt of the P38 stuffed into his waistband. The minutes ticked past. Tygo opened the front door and stepped outside through the covered porch. The sun was almost gone, the sky a purple bruise.

Snap! It was the sound of a hammer being flicked back on a pistol, and it was right behind him. He spun around and found himself facing the military policeman from the last checkpoint. He must have been hiding by the side of the porch.

"Take your pistol out and drop it on the ground."

Tygo thought about trying to talk his way out of it, but he could see that the man was deadly serious. He drew the Walther out of his waistband and let it fall to the ground. There was a round in the chamber and the safety was off; perhaps there was a way . . .

"Move!" The man spoke urgently but quietly. Tygo wondered where his partner was, why he hadn't heard their vehicle. The policeman was shoving him back into the house, the barrel of the gun jabbing Tygo's back.

"Stop," the policeman hissed, once they were in the hall. Before Tygo could say anything, Pieter suddenly appeared from the kitchen carrying a heavy-looking wooden box in both hands.

"Hey, Tygo, give your . . ." he began, then he saw the policeman and his voice died.

"Stay where you are!" the policeman barked. He put his arm around Tygo's neck and pulled it tight, jamming the gun into his cheek.

"Of course, no problem." Pieter stood there, holding the box.

Thank God, thought Tygo, Pieter hadn't said the word sister! As far as the policemen knew, it was just the two of them.

"Hans!" he yelled now. "Cover me!" He started to back out of the house, using Tygo as a shield. "You!" he said to Pieter. "Come to me, keep ahold of the box!"

Pieter walked toward them slowly as they stepped outside. When they were a few yards outside the policeman stopped.

"Hans, what are you doing hiding behind our car?" Pieter called out.

"Be silent!" the policeman ordered, but now Tygo knew where the other man was, and hopefully so did Alisa.

"Very slowly, put the box down," the policeman said.

Tygo felt the arm around his neck begin to relax. He glanced down on the ground and saw his pistol lying in the snow a few yards away. He looked back up and saw Pieter was staring at him as he lowered the box to the ground. He nodded his head ever so slightly.

"Okay, now put your hands up."

Pieter raised his hands in the air. Tygo saw a flicker of movement behind him in the house. So did the guard.

"Hey!" he said, letting go of Tygo's neck.

"Now!" yelled Pieter.

Tygo slammed his elbow back as hard as he could into the policeman's ribs and then dove to his left, rolling toward his pistol. As he did so, submachine guns burst into life. His right hand found the pistol, and he swung up and around onto one knee.

The first policeman was spinning back toward the car, his machine gun firing wildly into the air, his body bucking from the bullets hitting him. Tygo saw Alisa in the doorway, the Sten at her hip, her left hand gripping the magazine.

Pieter was lying flat in the snow.

The second policeman suddenly appeared from behind the car. He leaned forward on the hood, aiming his submachine gun. Tygo fired three shots; the last hit the policeman in the shoulder and he fell back, the machine gun sliding off the hood.

Pieter ran forward across the snow. The first policeman was lying still, dead. He reached the second one, who was on his back, pushing himself along the ground with his legs, one arm useless, but desperately trying to draw his pistol from his holster with his good arm.

"Stop, don't!" said Tygo, but the man continued.

"I said stop or I'll shoot." Tygo was almost pleading.

The man got the pistol free, raised it.

There was a single gunshot, but it wasn't Tygo's or the man's. A red hole the size of a cherry appeared in the man's forehead and he fell back, lying still. A crimson corona quickly haloed around his head.

Alisa was standing next to Tygo, smoke curling from the end of her Sten. She switched out the magazine, tossing the old one aside and slotting the new one in. She snicked the bolt. Her expression was blank.

"I was going to shoot," Tygo said thinly. Alisa nodded and put her arm around his shoulders. He thought he might cry.

"I'm sorry, it's my fault," said Tygo. "I didn't hear them coming."

Pieter joined them.

"They must have left their car up the track," said Alisa.

"We have to move fast," Pieter said. He appeared to be grinning. "We'll take their vehicle as well. Every cloud has a silver lining. We can double up the amount we can bring." Tygo was amazed at how relaxed Pieter was being, as if they were going on a picnic and there was extra ginger ale. "Come on now, help your sister!"

He set off at a jog up the farm track to retrieve the policemen's Kübelwagen. Tygo and Alisa ran back to the house.

Minutes later Tygo was loading cases of ammunition, grenades, and explosives into the trunk of the Opel. Alisa reappeared, carrying a couple of German MG 42 machine guns. Tygo took them and tried to find a space for them.

"Put them on the backseat," his sister said.

"Have you killed a lot of people?" Tygo asked as he slid the guns across the backseats.

Alisa took a moment to answer. "I've shot a lot of people. Don't know how many I've killed."

Tygo nodded. Alisa glanced down at the body of the dead policeman. He didn't look very old, in his twenties probably. He was somebody's son, perhaps even somebody's father.

"It's a terrible thing, Tygo, to take a person's life." Alisa's eyes were wet, but perhaps it was just the biting cold. "Maybe after tonight, if we succeed, then everyone can stop killing each other for good."

Tygo suddenly had an awful feeling inside, like a premonition. "Don't die, Alisa," he said, and he felt tears on his cheeks.

Alisa leaned forward and kissed him quickly on his forehead, like a mother.

"I won't."

23

Krüger left the girl under guard in his tent and headed through the trees to the radio truck. It was a few minutes before six o'clock, time for the hourly radio check with the Führer's convoy.

Krüger pulled himself up the metal ladder and into the back of the truck. It was warm inside from all the electronics and was lit with dull red bulbs screwed into the ceiling. Two radio operators were sitting on metal chairs, headphones over their ears and large, horn-shaped Bakelite microphones around their necks. The sound of constant radio traffic filtered in. Beside the radios were two Enigma machines.

Krüger checked his watch; the second hand was closing in on the twelve. He nodded to the operator, who flicked a couple of dials and then spoke into the microphone.

"New Moon calling Night Wolf, New Moon calling Night Wolf, are you receiving?"

There was crackle and a hiss of static. "Night Wolf receiving" came a voice back to them.

Krüger grabbed a set of headphones and a hand microphone.

"Night Wolf, this is New Moon, all is ready here, what is your position?" He let go of the transmit button and waited.

"This is Night Wolf." Krüger recognized Müller's voice through his headset. "We have stopped for refueling. ETA to New Moon is five hours. Five hours."

"Five hours—understand, Night Wolf. Radio check in one hour."

"Radio check in one hour, New Moon. Out."

Krüger took off the headphones. Five hours until the Führer arrived. Tygo had better be here in the next five hours, or everything he had planned was for nothing. No ranch, no pretty Argentinian wife, no pleasant hours relaxing by a swimming pool. Well, Krüger swore to himself, if Frettchen didn't appear, he would take great satisfaction in putting a bullet in that young girl's head before he made his own escape.

24

They dragged the two policemen into a ditch by the side of the house and drove the remaining short distance south toward the coast and the outskirts of Zandvoort. They didn't meet any patrols, and after turning off the main road they followed the narrow single lane surrounded by thick woods until they reached the bridge they'd spotted on the map. It had an old wooden sign marking it as the Red Shank Bridge; Red Shank was the name of a common wading bird in that area. Over the bridge the track continued, as did the woods, leading a couple of miles farther on to sand dunes and the beach. The trees were mostly pine, with some beech and spruce among them. The snow lay thick on the ground.

They unloaded the Opel first, carrying the weapons and ammunition down the side of the canal embankment next to the bridge, and stored them just underneath the first wooden bridge support. Tygo took a moment to look at the underside. It was a typical Dutch bridge, supported by wooden piles driven into the bottom of the canal, and the central span could be lifted to allow river traffic to pass. Not that there was any: The canal itself was frozen as hard as concrete.

After they had emptied the Opel, Pieter drove it across the bridge and parked it inside the trees a couple hundred yards beyond. Tygo helped Alisa unload the Kübelwagen, then took it across the bridge himself and drove it in next to the Opel.

He walked back across the bridge with Pieter, who was peering up at the night sky; what little moon there was lay shrouded in high cloud. "Dark, that's good," he said.

Tygo nodded. "How long have you and my sister been . . . you know?"

"A few months," Pieter replied.

"Oh," said Tygo. "Are you going to marry her?"

Pieter laughed softly. "We haven't discussed it. Do I have your permission?"

"It's not funny," said Tygo.

"No," said Pieter more seriously. "You're right, it's not. She's a very beautiful woman."

Their boots crunched on the snow as they walked. They were nearly halfway across. Pieter hurried forward and across to the side, leaning over and looking down.

"This support, I think—this is the one to set the charges on." Tygo leaned over the side of the bridge to look. "You think you could climb over and do it?"

Tygo found a foothold on the steel latticework running along the side of the bridge, and swung his leg over so he was straddling it. He looked down at the frozen white canal below.

"Yes, I think so," he said, "but it might be easier to climb along underneath."

"Whatever you want," said Pieter.

Tygo swung his leg back and dropped down to the ground. They walked on in silence until they reached the end of the bridge, where Alisa was waiting for them. Several other members of the group had arrived, including Ursula, Tygo noted. He thought she was looking a little scared now.

"All right," said Pieter. "Alisa, help your brother set the charges. Tygo knows where to plant it." He turned to the others. "The rest of you, get your weapons."

Tygo quickly crossed to Ursula's side. "Are you okay?"

"Why do you care?" Ursula said, then added, "I'm sorry, I didn't mean . . ."

"It's all right, I understand," Tygo replied. Now was not the time to make up.

He hurried back to his sister, and together they slid down the side of the bank beside the bridge. Tygo watched as she opened one of the boxes.

"I think it might be easier if I crawl through under the

bridge to the middle rather than climb over the side," he said. "It'll take longer, that's the only thing."

"Okay, Tygo, if you say so. We've still got time, I'm pretty sure."

She lifted out a block of what looked like putty. It was about the size of a shoe box and looked similar to the stuff Krüger had used on the safe that day in the Löwensteins' villa. She started to roll it across her thighs, turning it slowly into a sausage shape, twice its original length.

"Try to wedge it well in—next to the pilings." She handed it to Tygo.

"Isn't it dangerous?"

Alisa shook her head. "Only when you detonate it. It's actually very stable."

Tygo nodded and slung the length around his neck. It was rather heavy.

Alisa reached back into the box and took out a silver cylinder the size of a cigarette, with two little contacts at one end. "Blasting cap. Once you've got the explosives in place, stick this in at one end and attach this wire to the contacts on the end." She handed him a reel of two-ply wire, which he stuffed inside his jacket. As he did so, he remembered the Red Queen and felt for it in his pocket in a sudden panic. But it was still there, buried at the bottom underneath his filthy handkerchief. He'd twisted the pocket around for good measure to hold it secure. He would do this one last task and then he must be on his way, he thought. He wondered what time it was. Willa rushed back into his consciousness again. What was she doing? Was she all right?

"Tygo?" His sister nudged him.

"Okay," he said and took a deep breath. "Here goes." He pulled himself up onto the first wooden beam and started to climb through the mesh of cross-supports toward the center of the bridge. The frozen canal below dropped away from him as he worked his way along. The beams were freezing cold, but not icy, thank God, and he was able to keep a good grip on them. Once or twice he missed his footing and slid back, but he managed to recover on both occasions with nothing more serious than wounded pride.

He carefully slipped the explosive from around his neck and, bracing his legs against the supports, used both his hands to press along the cross-support running between the two wooden pilings. They anchored the mechanism that lifted the middle section up. Satisfied, Tygo pushed the blasting cap into one end and wound the wires around the contacts. He carefully made his way back to the side of the canal, paying out the wire from its reel as he went.

When he reached the end, he dropped down onto the canal embankment and handed the wire to Alisa. She spliced the ends on to the screw-down contacts of the detonator box.

"We're set," she said. As she spoke, they both heard a deep rumble coming toward them.

"Is it them?" said Tygo. The rumble was getting louder, fuller somehow.

"No, no . . ." Alisa pointed to the dark night sky. "It's up there. Listen." They both lay on the snowy bank and looked up at the sky. Sure enough, the noise grew louder and louder until there was a great droning and buzzing sound filling the night. Allied bombers on their nightly journey to flatten what little remained standing in Germany.

"There must be hundreds of them," said Tygo.

"Thousands," said Alisa.

"I wouldn't want to be under that."

"Me neither." She squeezed his hand softly. "Now go on, find Pieter, tell him we're ready."

Krüger had also heard the bombers overhead, their steel bellies filled with blockbuster bombs and "cookies" to lay waste to another German town. It was now nearly ten; at the last radio check Müller had reported the convoy as being ahead of schedule. Hitler would be here soon.

Which left him with the vexed question of Tygo's whereabouts. Something must have happened. He had had his radio operators call Headquarters; Krüger's vehicle had been reported as having passed a checkpoint around four o'clock, to the west of the city, and then nothing. The police at the checkpoint had also disappeared.

The policeman in Krüger didn't like the situation one bit.

Something had gone wrong, and when the Führer arrived he would be empty-handed. He felt panic filtering in, but fought to keep it at bay. Without that stone his future was bleak. He realized he would have to desert there and then, make a run for it, for Müller would most surely carry out his threat and have him shot. Damn Tygo, damn him, his life was in that stupid boy's hands now. There was nothing he could do but wait and hope he turned up. Perhaps he had gone off on some half-baked pursuit of his own, but if he really wanted to save himself and the girl, he was going about it the wrong way. For a terrible moment he entertained the possibility the little ferret was dead but then dismissed the thought; he was a survivor, that one. Like him.

Krüger stopped outside the aircrew's tent. Hans Bauer, the Führer's personal pilot, was part of the convoy coming from the Adlerhorst, but the copilot and navigator had been flown in with the weapon the previous night. They were both KG 200 personnel, recommended by their Oberstleutnant Baumbach, and the navigator was also a fully trained pilot.

Krüger wondered if it would be a good idea to have them bring the plane up to the edge of the airstrip, ready to go. Although the night was clear, who knew if a fog might roll in off the sea? On balance he decided it was the best thing to do. He pulled the tent flap back and stepped inside. The two men were seated around a small metal stove, warming their hands. A coffeepot sat on the round plate on the top. They stood and saluted.

"Gentlemen, I think, given the time, it would be wise of us to bring the Arado up to the strip."

"But Commander Bauer is not here yet."

"I am aware of that, but it is my judgment that the plane should be ready for takeoff as soon as the passengers arrive."

"Of course, Oberst, a very sensible suggestion. We can warm the engines, run the flight checks, top out the tanks if necessary."

"Very good, I will pass the order down. How long do you think it will take?"

"Half an hour, perhaps. The Kettenkrad will tow her into position."

Krüger saluted and left them to get on with it. The radio operators would make the hourly check with the convoy and, God willing, Tygo would appear with the diamond that the Führer had promised to present personally to Eva Duarte. Not that Krüger believed in God, but he had to keep telling himself that it was all going to work out somehow.

He walked back toward his tent, where he had the girl under guard. She was sitting on a stool by the tent's stove, warming her hands.

"Your boyfriend is cutting it fine."

"Oh, he'll be here," Willa said firmly, but Krüger could detect fear under the bravado. In spite of that, he desperately hoped she was right.

25

Tygo had just given the news to Pieter about the charges being ready when everything seemed to slow down and speed up at the same time. He was crouched down on the southern side of the road, just inside the tree line. The bridge was about thirty yards away.

"Listen," he said. "I have to go now . . . Willa . . ."

"What?" Pieter was only half listening. "Engines! I hear engines!" he yelled out.

"What?" said Tygo.

Sure enough, the sound of heavy engines—lots of them—could suddenly be heard through the trees. They were approaching fast, too.

"Get ready!" shouted Pieter.

"No," said Tygo. "No, I have to go, it's not fair."

The lead armored car's headlights suddenly cut through

the darkness as it thundered around the corner. Behind it came the other vehicles, engines revving loudly.

"Attack!" shouted Pieter. The lead armored car was fifty yards from their position. Somewhere behind in the convoy was the leader of the Third Reich himself.

"Attack, attack, attack!"

Back at the airstrip Krüger heard something distant coming through the trees. There was a metallic chatter, and then the clump of an explosion.

He pulled the girl to her feet, gripping her arm.

"Ow," she squealed.

"Silence!"

People always said machine-gun fire sounded like this or that. But it didn't. Machine-gun fire sounded like machine-gun fire, and that was what he could hear.

"Come with me." He pulled her out of the tent. "Lieutenant!" he bellowed.

A junior Luftwaffe officer came pelting through the night toward him.

"Yes, sir."

"Get the fires lit for the airstrip, take up defense positions!"

Ahead he could see the Arado gliding through the trees toward the runway. Krüger knew that the convoy must be under attack; it was too close to be anything else.

"It's Tygo! He's coming to get you," Willa yelled.

And suddenly Krüger realized she was probably right.

In fact, at that very moment Tygo was down on one knee firing a Sten gun toward the leading vehicle. The whole night had exploded with pyrotechnics. The other Resistance fighters had opened up with everything they had, the MG 42s sluicing rounds into the oncoming vehicles. Whether by luck or intention, they had managed to shoot out the tires on the front Puma, which skidded wildly off the side of the road and into the trees.

That left the leading Mercedes exposed. Bullets slammed into it, and a sheet of flame leapt up from the hood. The car stopped in the road. The second armored car pulled out from the back, managing to drive forward and place itself in front of the Mercedes to protect it. Its turret swung around, its flak cannons pumping cannon shells into the trees. At the back of the column, soldiers were dropping out of the truck, several falling to the ground, already cut down. The first Puma was also firing.

Pieter stood up and hurled a grenade toward it. "Get back to Alisa, tell her to blow the bridge—we can't hold this many for long."

Tygo got to his feet. There was so much noise now. Someone had fired a parachute flare and it lit up the night as it floated down. At least it meant he could see where he was going, but it also made him a sitting target. He felt several bullets zip past him. A cannon shell banged off the side of the bridge in a streak of sparks.

He fought to keep his footing on the snowy ground. The flare had gone out and there was darkness again. Tygo knew they would have to try to cross the bridge. He looked back. The army truck had pulled alongside the second Mercedes, the third armored car on the other side of it, boxing it in, protecting it. Maybe Pieter would try to outflank it. A long line of tracer suddenly pulsed above his head.

But then he had reached the bridge, was sliding down the embankment, gasping for air.

Alisa was there, waiting in the dark.

"Blow it, Pieter says to blow it now!" Tygo gasped.

Alisa raised the plunger on the detonator box and rammed it down. Nothing.

"Blow it!" yelled Tygo.

Alisa repeated the action. Nothing.

"What's wrong?"

"Oh no . . ." moaned Alisa. "The contacts on the blasting cap—a wire must have come loose."

Another cannon shell went past over their heads and banged off the metal latticework. Tygo could hear engines revving above the gunfire. Perhaps they were going to force their way across with the Mercedes in the middle like a Roman legion formation.

Unless someone fixed the charges, the opportunity would be lost and Hitler would escape, along with the wonder weapon. And Tygo knew that, however dangerous it was, there was only one person who could do that job.

"I'll go," he shouted, and scrambled back up the embankment. It would take too long climbing underneath as he had done before. He would have to run the gauntlet of the bridge itself and go over the side.

He reached the top. Pieter and the others were still keeping the convoy pinned down, but the lead armored car was slowly rolling forward. Scores of muzzle flashes danced in the darkness like fireflies.

"Someone cover me!" he yelled at the top of his voice. The bullets were fizzing past.

"I'll do it!"

It was a girl's voice. Ursula. She crawled across to him, a German MP 34 cradled in her arms. Tygo stared at her.

"Well, go on, before I change my mind!"

Tygo ducked low and ran as fast as he could down the bridge. Tufts of splintered wood appeared all around as he ran on, the whine of ricochets in the air. He glanced back; Ursula was hunched against the side of the bridge, firing at the convoy, edging closer.

Then the explosion. Tygo felt it before he heard it. It threw him forward, and he landed on his hands and knees. He glanced back; the fuel truck had exploded and an orange fire-ball had enveloped the vehicle. That should slow them down.

Ursula had turned at the head of the bridge to look for him, see if he was okay. He staggered up and waved back to her. Unfortunately, the light from the fire had picked him out, and as he ran to the middle stanchion a hail of bullets peppered the bridge. He heard Ursula returning fire. His heart was beating so hard in his chest, but there was nothing and nobody who would stop him. He reached the middle and looked back.

"No!" Ursula was down. Was she dead? Deep down, he knew she had to be. But there was nothing he could do. He'd be dead too if he didn't move fast.

He climbed over the side and, using his hands, let himself down until his legs caught ahold of the woodpile in front of him. Then he let go, sliding down the pile before wrapping his arms around it, breaking his descent. He swung around and braced himself; the explosive was still there, but the blasting cap had been pulled out. He must have tugged it out when he was paying the wire out earlier. He jammed the cap back deep into the C-3.

The firing was more sporadic now. He leaned out to see if he could see his sister.

"Alisa!" he yelled. He couldn't see anything. "I've done it! It's set!" he shouted at the top of his lungs.

He started climbing back to her, but then stopped. He had done everything he could to help the attack, and now it was time to think about saving Willa. He owed her that, and he had given his word. For the first time in a long time he was going to do something besides save his own skin.

Tygo turned around and started making his way to the other side of the bridge. He was over halfway there, and there was a good chance he could get to the other side before his sister blew the bridge. Once it was gone he'd never make it.

The armored car had stopped firing; perhaps it was out of ammunition. He hurried on, trying to pick his way through the timber maze in the dark and freezing cold. Another explosion rocked the night, more gunfire—sustained—engines revving. He couldn't see anything, could only listen to the sounds of battle. He was almost there now.

Tygo reached out for the next beam and found only air. It had been cut away for some reason. He plunged forward, losing his footing; there was nothing to grab, nothing to save him. He fell through the air, maybe four or five yards. He hit the ice feetfirst.

There was a terrific cracking noise, and then he was straight through the ice. It wasn't as thick as it looked. In an instant he was plunged into a pitch-black world of icy water. He thought his heart had stopped.

He had instinctively kicked up with his legs as soon as he was through the ice, knowing every second counted if he was to have any chance of living. He'd only been in the water for a few seconds, but he had to get his overcoat off before it dragged him to the bottom. The water was beyond cold; it felt like his chest was held in a vise. He shook the coat off one arm, then his head struck the ice. The current had already taken him past the hole he'd made.

He got his other arm out of the coat, feeling himself being carried away. How long had he been under—ten seconds? The top of his head was banging against the ice. Then his black world suddenly became light as an orange glow bathed the water around him.

He looked up and saw the light, bright for an instant through the ice, and realized in some separate compartment in his brain that Alisa must have blown the bridge. He gasped involuntarily and sucked in a lungful of freezing water. It felt like his lungs had burst into flames; he retched and sucked in more. *I'm drowning,* he thought, *I'm drowning . . .*

Twenty seconds.

A bridge timber support crashed through the ice in front of Tygo's face. Six inches closer and it would have been like a sledgehammer hitting a melon. Instead it saved his life, blasting a gigantic hole in the ice. His head broke the surface, and he was coughing and kicking through the water, the explosion and debris pulverizing the ice. The current had taken him almost to the other bank.

A few more kicks and he felt the side of the canal, pulled

himself up and onto the snow. He retched a couple more times; already his teeth were chattering. The gunfire kept up on the other side. He stared across—the bridge was gone. Totally gone.

He whooped as loud as he could. He yelled and danced and didn't care if it made him a target. Then he wove his way up the bank like a Friday-night drunk, collapsing on his knees at the top. He knew he should feel freezing, but he didn't feel cold at all—he felt great. He was alive, he was in one piece, he was in shock. He felt desperately sick; nevertheless, the adrenaline poured through his body and he staggered to his feet.

Tygo took one last look across the canal. The gunfire hadn't stopped; the armored car's engine was revving loudly and the convoy appeared to be reversing away from the bridge. He wondered briefly if the Führer was dead. *Please, God.* He wondered about Alisa too; she had to make it through.

He checked his pockets. *Thank God*—the stone was there, still twisted tightly up. He had to get to Willa. He turned and ran toward the trees. He found the Opel and threw himself behind the driver's seat. His teeth were still chattering and he was shaking all over. He twisted the key in the ignition; the engine turned over but didn't start. *Damn it.* It must be the cold.

He looked along the dashboard, his hands dancing around like a concert pianist's. He found the choke and eased it halfway out, very carefully; if he flooded the engine, he'd be done for. He turned the key again and the engine bit for a moment, then died.

Tygo pushed the choke back in and pumped the accelerator twice. *Last chance*, he thought: The battery was sounding very weak. He turned the key. The starter motor gave a pathetic little whir, but then the engine caught and fired. He gave the accelerator a thump, and the engine roared.

Tygo whooped with glee. Turning the heater up to full, he found first gear and let out the clutch. The car lurched forward through the trees. He changed into second and the big car hit the side of the lane. Hauling the wheel around, Tygo pointed it down the lane, getting the car into third. The speedo showed thirty-five miles per hour. He'd keep it in third and make it to the base in ten minutes.

26

Krüger had divided his time between listening to the fighting and making sure the plane was ready for an emergency take-off. This was an unparalleled disaster: The Führer's convoy was under attack from Resistance fighters. They had traveled so far, only to meet this outrageous assault so close to safety.

He tried to figure out where the fighting was. It seemed quite close; perhaps where the road became a single track before crossing the canal. That was a danger point. There had been an almighty explosion, and he thought the bridge must have been blown. His men in the radio truck could get nothing back from the convoy—not surprisingly, perhaps, during such intense fighting.

The Arado was now standing on the edge of the make-shift runway, its takeoff lights on. Other lights flickered from inside the cone-shaped cockpit as the copilot and navigator ran through their preflight checks. Everyone was on edge, the guards training their guns on the approach road.

Krüger glanced down the runway; men were lighting the buckets filled with oil-soaked rags, and an outline of the strip was appearing. More ground crew were lighting flares down the center line. Then through the woods he heard the sound of a vehicle, its engine straining as it raced along in a low gear.

"Hold your fire," he yelled to the itchy-trigger-fingered soldiers.

In less than a minute, he could see it was his Opel swerving and weaving along the track, and he immediately knew who would be driving it.

It skidded to a halt, almost colliding with a service truck. Krüger ran across to it, ripped open the driver's door. Sure enough, there was Tygo behind the wheel—shaking uncontrollably. He was soaked through.

Krüger pulled him by his soaking shirt from behind the wheel. "The stone, do you have the stone?" he yelled at him.

Tygo nodded. "Y-y-yes."

Krüger's heart jumped at the news. He let go of the boy. The stone was safe.

"What the hell has happened, Frettchen?" he demanded.

"C-c-cold," Tygo managed. His teeth were chattering badly now.

"Get me a blanket, dry clothes!" Krüger shouted; he didn't want him dead quite yet. By the car's interior light he could see that the young man's lips were blue; he was halfway there already. Krüger pulled out his hip flask and handed it to Tygo, who took a swig, then coughed. His teeth stopped chattering.

"Ambush on the convoy," Tygo managed to say.

A soldier ran up with a thick army blanket, a set of gray coveralls, and a field jacket. Krüger threw the blanket around Tygo's shoulders.

"What do you know about a convoy?"

"Know everything." His teeth continued to chatter. "H-H-Hitler in the c-c-convoy. The bridge has gone; they can't get across."

Krüger stood there and swore.

Tygo could see he was trying to figure out what to do; even in his befuddled state, he could understand that this changed everything for Krüger.

He watched the man pace in front of him. Finally he appeared to reach some sort of decision, and Tygo had another thought: Maybe this didn't change anything. Not for Krüger. He had the plane, and soon he'd have the stone too.

Yes, that was it: Krüger was almost smiling. "Give me the stone," he said, holding out his hand.

"Wait." Tygo's mind was also racing now, thinking out his options, going over the horse-trading that the stone now afforded him—well, him and Willa. The stone could be for them what it was going to have been for Krüger: their golden ticket, their passport to freedom.

"You can have it . . . on one condition."

"And what is that?"

"You take me and Willa with you on the plane."

"And what makes you think I'm going on that plane?" Krüger couldn't believe the boy's—what was the Jewish word?—chutzpah.

Tygo looked at him as he stripped off his wet clothes. He noticed that his skin was tinged with blue. "You think you know me—your Frettchen. But I know you too, Oberst."

Tygo suddenly felt unafraid of Krüger; it was funny standing there freezing to death but he had never felt more powerful, his courage bubbling up inside him.

"The mission is finished, but you still have a chance. Do you really want to stay in Amsterdam when the British and Americans arrive? You can escape tonight—you can even keep the stone now, the stone that woman wants, someone who can give whatever it is that you want in return. You'll never get a better chance."

Krüger stared back at Tygo. "You're a lot smarter than you look, Frettchen . . . very well, it's a deal. Now let me have it."

Tygo dug into his trouser pocket. He pulled out the Red Queen and held it up. Even with just the weak light from the car's blinkered headlamp, the stone flared with fire.

Krüger smiled broadly and stepped toward Tygo. Tygo backed away.

"No!" he said and closed his fist. "One more step and it's gone forever."

Krüger put up his hands. "What's wrong? Surely you trust me."

"Don't treat me like a fool."

"You're right. The time for games is over." Krüger had his gun out of his holster in an instant, but before he could shoot, Tygo dropped the diamond into his mouth and swallowed.

"Your move," he said.

For a moment Krüger contemplated shooting the boy dead and retrieving the stone the bloody way with his SS ceremonial dagger. But no. Truth be told, a part of him almost admired Tygo's spirit. Perhaps he would even find a use for him if they made it out of there tonight.

A soldier sprinted across to them. "Oberst Krüger! I have General Müller on the shortwave. He needs to talk to you immediately!"

Krüger swore, then turned and ran back with the operator toward the radio truck, leaving Tygo pulling on the coveralls and flak jacket. There was nowhere for him to go from here—and Krüger still had the girl.

Krüger pulled himself up the metal ladder and into the

back of the truck. The two operators were waiting for him; they were quite young, and they looked scared.

"General Müller," one of them said, and handed a pair of headphones and microphone to Krüger.

Krüger grabbed them. "General Müller, this is Krüger. What is your situation?" It was too late for call signs.

Müller's voice came on the line. "The Führer is safe; we are withdrawing under fire. Reinforcements are on their way. Over."

"Understood, Herr General. What are your orders?"

"Hold flight time, repeat, hold flight time. We will be with you by zero six hours."

Krüger stood there, his mind racing. Six a.m.—that would mean flying across Europe in daylight, a near-suicidal proposition. Müller and Bormann must be desperate, he thought.

"Sorry, Herr General, say again?" Krüger waited.

"Zero six hours!" Müller's voice was louder in his earphones.

Krüger had the plane ready to go, protected by the night. Most important, he had the stone—or rather, he had Tygo, who had the stone. He could get to Argentina—give it to Eva Duarte himself . . .

"I understand, Herr General. We will carry out the mission as planned."

"What are you talking about?" Müller was yelling.

"I'm losing you, Herr General, transmission is breaking up."

"Oberst Krüger, I am ordering you . . ."

Krüger pulled off the headphones and tossed them back to the radio operator.

"I lost him."

One of the operators glanced at the other one skeptically. "Are you sure, sir? I can try to reconnect you."

"No need, Corporal, I have my orders: The mission is to go ahead as scheduled. In fact, I think it would be a good idea"—Krüger slid his pistol from his holster—"if we observed radio silence from now on." He raised the pistol and fired. Eight shots. The operators would not be sending or receiving any time soon.

Krüger climbed out of the truck and closed the door firmly behind him. "Lieutenant!" he yelled, seeing the young commander of the Luftwaffe regiment. Krüger dropped out the clip on his Sauer 38H and slapped in a fresh magazine.

The lieutenant ran across. He looked worried, and his cap was gone.

"Lieutenant, I have just received orders from General Müller that we are to take off immediately. Once we are airborne, abandon the base and set demolition charges."

The lieutenant saluted and Krüger hurried past him. Sporadic gunfire could still be heard through the trees. Tygo was nowhere to be seen, but Krüger was not worried; he knew he was blundering about searching for Willa.

He ran up the ramp into the plane, making his way past the rocket and wooden crate, securely lashed down in the middle of the cargo bay, and past the private compartment specially fitted for the Führer until he reached the cockpit.

"Gentlemen," Krüger shouted, "there has been a complication, but the Führer has personally ordered us to take off immediately; the safe delivery of the T-Waffe to the U-boat is paramount. Are you able to do so?"

The copilot nodded. "Of course—we have both flown this bird before. We will start the engines."

"Excellent!" Krüger smiled. "Five minutes, we go in five minutes."

"You will act as the loadmaster?" the copilot shouted back to Krüger.

"*Ja*, I will do it," he replied, then turned and ran back down the plane. Stopping by the top of the ramp, he checked over the metal control panel that controlled the ramp and door hydraulics.

Tygo was searching the tents in the darkness, calling Willa's name loudly.

The lieutenant ran toward him. "Who are you?"

"Tygo Winter; I work for the Oberst."

"Have you seen him?" The lieutenant seemed panicked. "The radio operators have been shot!"

"No." Tygo ran on, dodging others in the dark. "Willa! Willa!"

He heard the engines start to turn over just as he reached the next tent. The flap flew back and Willa ran out and straight to him. They hugged tightly.

"I knew you'd come back," she said, kissing his cheek.

"We're getting on that plane to Barcelona. It's all going to work out, like I said."

"Tygo, *nothing's* worked out like you said."

"We're still here, aren't we?" Tygo's excitement was infectious. He took her hand. The plane's engines were building.

"Wait," said Willa. "There's something I don't understand. You brought the stone back, yes?"

Tygo nodded.

"Then why didn't he just take it and kill you?"

"Oh, he'd have liked to do that, but then how could I have saved you?"

Willa jabbed him in the ribs.

"Let's just say I thought of a very good reason why he had to take me, take *us* . . . we're going to escape this place, Willa. I think you'll like Barcelona. It's a nice city."

"Tygo, you're . . ." Willa was lost for words.

"Tell me later."

They ran together through the gloom toward the Arado. The camp was in chaos, soldiers collapsing tents and loading equipment. They were nearly at the ramp when Willa fell heavily.

She cried out, and when Tygo went to help her, he could see she had tripped over a body lying on the frozen ground. Tygo crouched down; it was the lieutenant, executed with a bullet to the head.

"Is he dead?" asked Willa, getting up onto her knees.

"Yes," said Tygo. The man's eyes were staring up at him unblinkingly, still with a look of surprise.

Krüger was taking no chances anymore.

Willa stood up. The plane's engines were blowing a back-draft through the trees toward them, sending pine needles and snow into their faces. "Come on, Tygo!" she shouted above the roar.

"Just a second." Tygo felt his way down the man's torso until he found his leather holster. He unclipped it and slid out the pistol. It was a Mauser HSc, a standard Luftwaffe sidearm. He stuffed it into the pocket of his field tunic. "Coming."

He grabbed Willa's hand, and they made it the short distance to the plane and scrambled up the ramp. There was no one inside. They stood there, catching their breath; the whole plane was now vibrating from the spinning propellers straining to be set free.

Willa glanced at the sleek, gray rocket strapped inside and the heavy wooden crate beside it. "Do you really think it's true what Krüger said, that this bomb can destroy all of New York City?"

Tygo looked at her. "He said that?"

Willa nodded. Tygo looked at the rocket, then at the wooden crate. "Well . . . I mean, look at what they've done to get this bomb and the Führer to safety . . . they *must* believe it will end the war." He was pulling Willa farther inside, toward the missile.

"But New York—that means it could kill millions."

"Do you really think that's true?"

Willa nodded. Tygo looked at the wooden crate again. The numbers on the side matched the numbers he had seen when he had stolen into Krüger's office and examined the secret file: *Ur 234 Spezielle Formul.*

"We can't let that happen, Tygo, we just can't."

"What are you saying, Willa . . . ?"

"Get inside!" It was Krüger, sprinting up the ramp, finishing Tygo's sentence for him. Despite the cold he was sweating heavily. Tygo noticed his holster was open, and he was carrying the leather valise from his office, no doubt containing the diamonds and all his other loot—share certificates, Swiss francs, gold sovereigns.

"Get to your seats. This plane is taking off!" Krüger pressed the control panel, and the ramp started to retract back up.

Tygo and Willa hurried through the cargo bay. Willa stopped when they reached the rocket. She ran her hand along the side of it, right up to the nose cone with its yard-long air speed tube attached to it like a rapier.

"It's evil," she said, and Tygo pulled her forward away from it.

They found a pair of seats bolted to the floor behind the private compartment. They slid in side by side, breathing hard. Tygo could see the plane's wing above them through the window, and one of the engine's exhaust spurting flecks of flame as they revved up.

He glanced back; the ramp was up, and the outer doors were closing over it. Krüger had the plane's intercom headphones on and was talking into the loadmaster's microphone box next to the hydraulics.

Tygo felt the brakes being released with a jolt, and the Arado moved forward. He leaned out and saw the pilots inside the cockpit; both had their hands over the four throttle levers between their two seats. The plane slowly started to gather speed, bumping over the metal panels that made up the airstrip.

Krüger hurried past them. "Go, go!" He yelled the order into the cockpit, opened the door to the private compartment just behind it, and disappeared inside.

Tygo looked out through the window. The plane's underwing lights had come on, and he noticed for the first time a large metal cylinder tapering to one end, about the size of a beer barrel. It was attached to a metal pod between the nacelles of the engines. As he stared at it, he realized something.

Willa was right: They couldn't let the Nazis use that weapon. They had the power to stop them . . . but that power was right now. Not in six hours' time when they landed in Barcelona; by then it would be too late. He had to forget this idealized picture he had of Willa and himself sitting on a beach in Spain, waiting for the war to end. It really was now or never.

Pieter and his sister had stopped the Führer from escaping; Tygo and Willa would stop him from winning the war. It was as simple as that. He had to stop the plane from taking off; if he could do that, he and Willa still had a chance of getting away through the woods. There was only Krüger who would care.

He undid his seat belt.

"What are you doing?" Willa asked.

"You said it yourself, Willa, we can't let the Nazis use that weapon. We've got to stop them!"

"But how . . ."

"I've got the pistol, remember? It's risky, but . . ."

Suddenly there was an explosion from outside the window. A sheet of flame had shot out of the end of the cylinder, and it was as if a giant had picked up the plane like a paper dart and hurled it forward. They would be airborne in seconds, Tygo realized.

"Yes or no, Willa?"

"Okay, yes, yes!"

Tygo jumped out of his seat and ran forward toward the cockpit. The floor was rising as he ran, and he felt the nose wheel of the aircraft suddenly lift off the ground. He struggled forward. The auxiliary rocket boosters under the plane's wings were blasting it into the air; he wasn't going to make it. He felt the back wheels come off the ground. Just a few more steps. The plane was climbing now, banking sharply.

He grabbed ahold of the bulkhead at the entrance to the cockpit, drawing his pistol. Alisa was right, it was terrible thing he was about to do, but he had no choice. He fired.

The pilot was leaning forward out of his seat, keeping the pressure up on the engine throttles. Tygo's first three shots hit him in the back, throwing him forward onto his control wheel. The navigator, now acting as the copilot, turned around in his seat, and Tygo fired again. The bullet caught the man high up, shattering his collarbone, and spun him back.

The plane suddenly pitched forward and started to dive. Tygo hung on to the side of the bulkhead. Behind him, the door to the private compartment slammed open and Krüger braced himself in the door frame.

"Frettchen!" he screamed. "What have you done?" He fumbled for his pistol as the plane dipped lower, the auxiliary rockets under the wings now spent of fuel.

The navigator was back up, pulling on the wheel weakly with one hand, the other pushing the engine's throttles back toward idle. The nose lifted and they seemed to be flying horizontally now. The plane's landing lights were still on, and Tygo stared ahead wide-eyed through the conical Perspex dome of the cockpit. He saw the dunes flash by just below them, then a strip of white sand, concrete and metal blocks and spikes sprouting from it, a ribbon of gray surf.

Then the plane drove into the black water beyond, and the Perspex windows imploded. A wall of water hit Tygo in an instant and hurled him into oblivion.

27

For a moment Tygo wondered if he was dead, then the icy water lapping around him dragged him fully conscious. He must have been out for only a couple of minutes. He tried to get his bearings; he was tangled up in the metal seats on the other side of the fuselage from Willa and the private compartment. The red running lights along the side of the fuselage were still working, giving the inside a hellish red glow.

There was something sticky on his face, and when he put his hand to it, it came away crimson. He was bleeding, but he didn't feel any pain. He looked around, trying to clear the fuzziness from inside his head.

The plane appeared to have crashed into shallow water just beyond the surf line of the beach. It had gone nose in, and the cockpit had been shattered as it hit the bottom of the seabed, water pouring in. The initial onrush was what had thrown

Tygo back, but now the plane had settled and was lying at a twenty-degree angle into the water. The cockpit remained completely flooded. Tygo glanced out the windows; the rockets had burned out, but some of the engines were still running. Flames were starting to lick around one of them, and there was a strong smell of burning rubber and fuel.

Tygo slowly disentangled himself. Quite apart from the missile, which appeared to still be secured to the floor of the plane, they were inside what was potentially a massive bomb once the fuel tanks caught.

"Willa!" he cried. Her seat was on the other side of the rocket. He could see her lying there, unconscious. He pulled himself to his feet and, using the rocket to hold on to, started to make his way back up the plane. The whole fuselage was gradually filling with water.

There was no sign of Krüger. Tygo hoped he'd broken his bloody neck.

Tygo edged around the back end of the rocket, then sat down and slid all the way along the floor of the plane, down to where he could see Willa slumped in her seat. He hoped *she* hadn't broken her neck! The water was up to her knees, and Tygo had to grab the chair's frame to stop himself from slipping. It was freezing cold too. He took ahold of Willa's shoulder and shook it.

"Willa! It's me, Tygo . . . Wake up."

She gave a moan, and then slowly opened her eyes. Tygo saw that she had a cut above one of them, and a line of blood had slid down one cheek. He scooped up some of the water in his hand and chucked it at her face. She moaned again, but at least he'd washed the blood off.

"We've crashed, Willa. We have to get out of here before it explodes, do you understand me?"

Just then, he heard the dull crump of petrol igniting some-where. Through the window he saw the nearside engine enveloped in flame.

"Can't," said Willa, trying to push him away.

Tygo leaned forward and released her waist belt. She started to slide out of the seat, and he caught her under her arms. "Please, Willa, you have to help me." He let go with one of his hands and slapped her across the cheek. The water con-tinued to rise. He dragged her forward off her chair, and she managed to find her legs, coming awake now.

"Okay, Tygo," she said weakly. "I'm trying . . ."

"Hold my arm, don't let go . . ." Tygo grabbed ahold of the chair frames with one hand, keeping hold of Willa with the other. Slowly he began to pull them both up the plane toward the exit ramp. The whole cabin was starting to fill with acrid smoke, but as the water continued to rush in, it was start-ing to act like a counterweight, leveling the plane out. It made it a little easier to climb.

When they reached the rocket, Tygo used the thick canvas straps that had been employed to lash it down to keep pulling them up. The seawater was creeping all the way up the plane, faster and faster, and the angle it was resting at was starting to drop more and more. They kept going; they needed to get the ramp down and be out of there before the whole cargo area flooded to the ceiling. But maybe it didn't matter, thought Tygo: The plane would probably have exploded by then. It sounded like an engine on the other side had just caught fire.

Finally they reached the ramp. The running lights were still on; Tygo prayed there was still power to the hydraulics and they would work. He pressed the black knob marked *Öffnen* on the control panel. There was a whining sound, followed by a grinding one, and then the outer doors started to swing back and the cold night air rushed into the smoke-filled compartment. Relief washed over Tygo. Now they just had to get the ramp down.

He glanced down to check on Willa; she was slumped against the side of the fuselage. He leaned down and lightly slapped her face. "Willa? Come on, we're nearly free."

She took his hand. "It's okay, I'm all right . . . We did it, Tygo."

Then she opened her eyes wider and let out a piercing scream.

Tygo turned just in time to see a flash of steel and fling himself to the side. The ax-head embedded itself in the soft metal skin of the fuselage.

Krüger was holding on to the handle, frantically trying to pull it out. His eyes were wild with rage, his tunic ripped to shreds, his face ribboned with blood. He looked demonic in the red light as he kept pulling at the ax-head, working to get it free.

Tygo charged toward him, using the angle of the plane to his advantage. He slammed into Krüger with his shoulder at waist height, and Krüger lost his grip on the ax. The two of them fell back, landing on the cargo bed, and started to tumble down the length of the plane, trading blows and kicks as they did.

They careened past the rocket and warhead and plunged back into the rising water, disappearing beneath the surface. Krüger was the first to emerge, blowing water from his mouth; he staggered up the fuselage, but Tygo surfaced seconds later. He clambered back out and the two of them faced each other on opposite sides of the fuselage. The door to the private compartment was hanging off its hinges.

Tygo looked at Krüger. Neither of them was armed, except with their fists and feet and teeth. But whatever happened, only one of them was going to live.

"Why?" yelled Krüger. "Why?"

Flames were licking along the cabin roof above their heads, the paint blistering and steam hissing. The smoke bit at Tygo's throat.

"What was I supposed to do? Let you blow up a city, murder all those people?"

"What you were supposed to do was survive, you fool, survive! That was the plan. How many million people are dead already? What's a few more to add to the pile?"

Krüger threw himself at Tygo, swinging his fists. His right caught Tygo's chin, and he fell back against the side of the private compartment. Krüger grabbed him and pinned him there, his hand around Tygo's neck. Very slowly he eased him up the metal-skinned wall, till Tygo's feet were kicking free of the floor.

From higher up the fuselage came a sharp clang of metal striking metal. Neither of them looked to see what was making the noise. Tygo couldn't, and Krüger was too focused on the task at hand.

"You know," he whispered, "this is the best way to kill a ferret, by wringing its neck."

Tygo's face felt as if it were on fire, inside his brain was pounding, and his ears felt like they would burst. Big red dots swam in front of his eyes. He tried to swing his fists at Krüger, but the Oberst batted them away easily. There was another clang of metal on metal. Tygo was starting to lose consciousness; a black curtain was drawing across in front of his eyes.

"Tygo!" Willa screamed his name. It brought him back for an instant, and he looked up the plane. So did Krüger.

Willa raised the ax above her head and slammed it down. It severed the last remaining canvas strap securing the rocket to the floor of the plane. It shot forward toward them.

Krüger let go of Tygo in alarm, and Tygo leaned against the wall. He raised his right leg. The missile was hurtling down. Tygo kicked out and hit Krüger in the stomach.

Krüger staggered back, realized where the kick had put him, and screamed in fear.

The rapier tube on the front of the rocket ran him through, straight through the middle of his torso. He grabbed helplessly at it, but the rocket kept going, driving him and itself beneath the water and into the bowels of the submerged plane. Krüger was gone. For good.

Tygo struggled back up the plane. The engines were well on fire by now. Willa was waiting for him by the wooden crate, still holding the fire ax.

"You saved my life," he croaked.

"Not if we don't get out of here soon," Willa said, and she took his arm and pulled him toward the ramp.

He grabbed the control button and pressed it. There was no response. He pressed it frantically. "We've lost the hydraulics," he said.

Willa glanced around. "Look." She pointed to a metal handle secured to a bracket on the side. It was a hand winch.

Tygo ripped it free and searched for the bolt head to fit it onto. There it was, on the other side. He slid the handle on and started to crank it. The ramp dropped down a little bit. It would take a while to get it completely open.

"Just open it enough so we can crawl out," Willa shouted, clearly thinking the same thing.

Tygo kept on turning, and the ramp dropped away until he stopped, and the two of them clambered up it and fell over the side into the water below.

It was the second time that night he'd been dunked in freezing water, but Tygo still couldn't get used to it. His head broke the surface, but he couldn't draw breath—or rather, all he could do was draw breath—he couldn't exhale. Willa's head burst through the surface next to him. The beach was about twenty yards from them. Tygo took in a big gulp of seawater, coughing.

"We can make it, Tygo . . . Kick, kick hard," Willa urged him on as he floundered.

The two of them struck out toward the beach. The tide was with them, a strong, new-moon tide pushing them in on the surf. The water crashed over Tygo's head, the undertow pulling at his legs. Tygo felt himself going under, swallowing water, then Willa grabbed his hair and yanked his face back above the surface.

"Keep going, Tygo!"

He found the last of his strength and kicked hard. Ten yards out, they touched bottom and could stand. They waded in from there.

The flames from the burning plane lit up the sand. Both of them dropped to their knees. Tygo suddenly felt terribly nauseous. He retched, the seawater coming back up, a horrible sour, briny taste. He retched again, felt something hard in his throat, gagged. The Red Queen shot out of his mouth and lay on the sand.

Willa crawled over to him. "What's that?"

Tygo grabbed the stone and rinsed it in the shallow water. It glittered in the light of the burning plane. Willa stared at it, then at Tygo. "You swallowed it?"

"Seemed a good idea at the time. Here, take it; it's yours."

Willa looked at it for a moment or two. "I don't want it, Tygo." She looked back at the plane. "Come on, we need to get out of here, that bomb . . ."

"You must take it. It's yours, it's priceless."

"Not to me."

"But it's your future . . ."

"Now you sound like him, like Krüger."

Tygo dropped his head. "You're right. I'm sorry."

Willa leaned over and folded his fingers back around the stone. "Why don't you look after it for me, Tygo, keep it safe?"

Tygo smiled. "I can do that. I can absolutely do that."

"Right, now can we get out of here?"

Tygo nodded and climbed unsteadily to his feet.

"Come, I'll race you to the woods!" Willa made it sound like they were on a day out to the beach.

"I can't . . ." Tygo felt dizzy.

"Don't tell me the great Tygo Winter is giving up?"

Tygo stared at her, her blond hair plastered flat against her porcelain skin, her topaz eyes staring down at him. They were no longer filled with fear as they had been when he had first looked into them. Now they were smiling at him.

"Never," he croaked.

She took his hand and pulled him forward, and they started to run along the sand.

Behind them the plane was engulfed in flames, like some Viking sacrifice.

28

At 2:57 a.m. the Nazis' first and only nuclear bomb exploded inside the burning wreckage of the Arado, almost six months to the day before the Americans' Trinity test in Nevada.

The Führer's convoy had successfully retreated back onto the main road to Haarlem. The vehicles were grouped together, their engines running. When the bomb had exploded, the light had illuminated the line of cars as if a battery of searchlights had been parked in front of it and switched on. Then a roaring wind had hit them, filled with dust, sand, leaves, sticks . . . anything that could be picked up and hurled their way. It was accompanied by a sound like a dozen express trains driving straight through them.

Müller staggered forward to the Führer's car, his eyes still dazzled. He had failed to reach Krüger on the radio for the last hour, and now he knew why. In the distance was a column of smoke.

He reached the car; Bormann stared out at him from the back. He put up his hand for Müller to wait. Müller caught a glimpse of the Führer; his face was incandescent with rage. After several minutes the passenger door opened and Bormann climbed out.

"Did you see the power of it?" Müller shouted, his ears ringing.

"Yes, truly it is a wondrous weapon. Once again, the Führer's genius has been demonstrated." He shook his head bitterly. "And once again his trust has been betrayed!" He swore loudly, using every filthy word he could think of.

Müller waited until he had finished. "What are the Führer's orders?"

"Operation Black Sun is finished. The plane is gone, the bomb is gone. Now it is the Führer's wish to continue the fight from Berlin."

"We can get another plane," said Müller. "There are more bombs."

"It is too late now. The Führer has decided: He will stay and fight, fight until victory is achieved."

"But that is impossible."

"Those are the Führer's orders." Müller could see that Bormann felt the same.

"Of course." Müller nodded. It was all over now. Time for him to make his own separate travel plans.

Pieter and Alisa had made it to the outskirts of Haarlem when the whole night lit up for an instant, like a switch had been thrown from above. The street they were standing in was suddenly washed white, and then the darkness returned, accompanied by a murderous thunder rolling toward them.

"What was that?" said Alisa.

Pieter shook his head and coughed again, tasting blood.

"Whatever it was, it's gone now," he said. He was feeling light-headed from the loss of blood. He sagged against Alisa, and she caught him, pulling one of his arms over her shoulders to support him. He was a dead weight.

"No, don't you dare!" she said. "Big strong brute like you . . . We're nearly there." The safe house was in the next street. She would call a doctor; he would take care of Pieter. She would save him, like he had saved her.

"Come on, now." Alisa started to sing softly to him. "Poor old man . . ."

At first light, Tygo and Willa found a gap in the barbed wire and made their way up through the dunes. The sand was rock hard, covered in snow, and the tufted grass that grew on the hillocks was iced with frost.

They were glad that hellish night was finally over, but neither of them would ever forget the moment when the darkness had turned to a searing white light. The roaring blast of the wind, throwing them to the ground, the sound like the earth being torn apart.

Shaken, they had gotten back to their feet and seen in the distance a tall, thin column of smoke rising up in the dark sky, the top of it forming the shape of a mushroom. It was horribly beautiful.

"Do you want to rest?" Tygo asked.

"No, I'm okay." Willa took his hand. Her fingers were freezing. *Cold hands, warm heart*, that was what they said. In Willa's case Tygo was sure it must be true.

"Look, what's that?" Willa pointed to something farther up on the beach.

Tygo squinted. "It's a little boat!" he exclaimed. He sprinted down through the dune on to the beach. Willa ran after him.

The two of them examined it. It was a clinker-built skiff with a bench seat in the middle, and a little mast with a tatty sail forward of that. Tygo looked inside.

"There's a pair of oars." He looked at Willa, excited. "Let's see if it's seaworthy."

The two of them pushed the boat down into the surf. The icy water bit into their feet and shins.

"Seems sound enough to me," Tygo said. "Come on."

He helped Willa clamber on board, then pulled himself in. He fit the oars into the boat's rowlocks.

"Where are we going?"

"Wherever we want," Tygo replied with a grin.

And with that, the two of them dropped their oars into the water and heaved.

HISTORICAL NOTE

As you may have realized, this is a work of fiction, and of course none of what takes place in the plot actually occurred, although some things in the story are true.

The Winter of Hunger was a very real event for the brave people of the Netherlands, and many thousands died of malnutrition, cold, and disease. Many were also shot for their Resistance work or in reprisal actions. Although the south of the country was liberated by the end of 1944, Amsterdam and the north were not freed from the Nazi yoke until May 1945.

The guns, planes, and cars used in the story are all accurate, except for the T-Waffe weapons that were loaded on the plane at the end. However, more primitive versions almost certainly existed, including many different types of rockets and missiles. It is generally believed that the Nazis had some nuclear capability by the end of the war, and there is a school of thought that argues that the nuclear material inside the Little Boy, the bomb the Americans dropped on Nagasaki, was in fact captured from a Nazi U-Boat 234 at the end of the war. Reports also exist of the Nazis testing such a weapon on the island of Rügen in the Baltic in late 1944, and in Thuringia in March 1945. Furthermore, there are a number of sources that suggest that nuclear weapons were being made at the Gusen concentration camp near St. Georgen.

In particular, much mystery remains about an enormous secret weapon project called the "Bell." It is believed to have been some sort of anti-gravity device, and perhaps is the reason for so many reports of flying disks and flying balls by Allied pilots at the end of the war. They gave rise to the nickname "foo fighters," based on the French word *feu*, meaning "fire." Modern stealth and drone technology is directly attributable to these experimental designs and prototypes.

Of the people in the story:

GENERAL "GESTAPO" HEINRICH MÜLLER

General Müller was head of the Gestapo to the very end of the war. He escaped from Hitler's bunker in Berlin and disappeared as the Soviets closed in. It is generally believed he survived the war and either went to work for the Americans or the Soviets, depending on whose propaganda and counter-propaganda you believe.

HAN VAN MEEGEREN

Van Meegeren was a celebrated Dutch forger and art dealer who was put on trial by the Dutch authorities after the war for his forgeries of Vermeer paintings. He managed to make himself something of a folk hero from the case, claiming that by making the Nazis pay a fortune for his works he was contributing to the war effort.

WERNER BAUMBACH

Baumbach was a highly decorated Luftwaffe pilot and one of the commanders of the special operations flight known as KG 200. Baumbach really did fly captured American planes and other very specialized craft, and was involved in many secret missions. He survived the war, and even wrote a book about his life without ever mentioning the KG 200 air squadron.

EVA DUARTE

She became, on October 18, 1945, the wife of General Perón, who was vice president of Argentina in January 1945. He later became president of the country in 1946. It is widely known that both he and previous regimes were pro-Nazi (despite having declared war on Germany at the beginning of 1945) and that vast amounts of money and gold were transferred to German companies set up in Argentina by Martin Bormann. A great number of ex-Nazis settled there comfortably after the war—including, if you choose to believe alternative history books, Martin Bormann, and even Adolf Hitler himself.

EVA BRAUN

She was Hitler's longtime mistress. He married her in the bunker in Berlin on April 29, 1945, and they committed suicide together the following day. Her sister Gretl Braun survived the war and died in 1987.

When researching this novel, I found these books really useful: *The Man Who Made Vermeers* by Jonathan Lopez; *KG 200: The Luftwaffe's Most Secret Unit* by Geoffrey J. Thomas & Barry Ketley; *The Hunger Winter* by Henri A. van der Zee; *Nazi Looting: The Plunder of Dutch Jewry during the Second World War* by Gerard Aalders; *The Real Odessa: How Perón Brought the Nazi War Criminals to Argentina* by Uki Goni; *The Truth About the Wunderwaffe* by Igor Witkowski; and *Emmy Andriesse—Photographs 1944/52* by Emmy Andriesse.

ACKNOWLEDGMENTS

This is like the end of a film when the credits roll and everyone leaves. For the odd few who stay to the copyright and Panavision logos, here are the people I would like to thank for helping me with this story. My mother and father, who both served during the war. My wonderful wife and four gorgeous children. Michael, Nelda, and Judy, who know who they are and what they do! Major Von Hapen; my fabulous editor, Rachel, who is an alchemist; Barry, my amazing boss; the other incredible Rachel; and of course everyone else at Chicken House, which is the best publisher in the galaxy. Thank you, one and all.

ABOUT THE AUTHOR

William Osborne became a lawyer after graduating from Cambridge University, but his career took a sharp turn when he switched to screenwriting in Hollywood. He has worked on more than sixty movies, including *The Mummy* and *GoldenEye*. His first novel, *Hitler's Secret*, was longlisted for the prestigious Carnegie Medal in the United Kingdom. He lives in Norfolk, England.